"We need to establish some goalpost, guidelines…" What was she trying to say? "We need to work out the rules."

"Rules?" Pasco asked, his expression derisive.

Aisha dropped her hand to nail him with a hard look. "Yes, I know, you are a hotshot chef who doesn't think rules apply to him, but with our history and if we are going to be working together, then we need some."

"There's only one rule…" Pasco told her, hands on his hips. "Do what I want, when I want it and we'll get along fine."

Aisha clenched her fists, her fingernails digging into her palms. A part of her suspected he was teasing her, but she couldn't back down, be seen as weak. If she did, Pasco would gobble her up and spit her out. Not happening. "You really should see somebody to talk about your delusions of grandeur, Kildare."

She saw a gleam in his eyes she didn't like but decided to ignore it. "That tongue of yours has got sharper, Aisha Kildare…"

Joss Wood loves books and traveling—especially to the wild places of southern Africa and, well, anywhere. She's a wife, a mom to two teenagers and a slave to two cats. After a career in local economic development, she now writes full-time. Joss is a member of Romance Writers of America and Romance Writers of South Africa.

Books by Joss Wood

Harlequin Presents

South Africa's Scandalous Billionaires

How to Undo the Proud Billionaire
How to Win the Wild Billionaire
How to Tempt the Off-Limits Billionaire

Harlequin Desire

Reckless Envy
Hot Holiday Fling
At the Rancher's Pleasure
Homecoming Heartbreaker
How to Handle a Heartbreaker

Visit the Author Profile page
at Harlequin.com for more titles.

Joss Wood

THE RULES OF THEIR RED-HOT REUNION

HARLEQUIN®
PRESENTS®

Recycling programs for this product may not exist in your area.

ISBN-13: 978-1-335-56929-5

The Rules of Their Red-Hot Reunion

Copyright © 2021 by Joss Wood

All rights reserved. No part of this book may be used or reproduced in any manner whatsoever without written permission except in the case of brief quotations embodied in critical articles and reviews.

This is a work of fiction. Names, characters, places and incidents are either the product of the author's imagination or are used fictitiously. Any resemblance to actual persons, living or dead, businesses, companies, events or locales is entirely coincidental.

This edition published by arrangement with Harlequin Books S.A.

For questions and comments about the quality of this book, please contact us at CustomerService@Harlequin.com.

Harlequin Enterprises ULC
22 Adelaide St. West, 40th Floor
Toronto, Ontario M5H 4E3, Canada
www.Harlequin.com

Printed in U.S.A.

THE RULES OF THEIR
RED-HOT REUNION

CHAPTER ONE

Walking down the stone pathway bisecting the emerald green swathe of grass, Aisha Shetty sent Ro Miya-Matthews's huge stomach a worried look. They'd just left the St Urban manor house, which would, under Aisha's direction, become a six-star boutique.

Enchanted that this amazing two-hundred-year-old building was going to be her base for the foreseeable future—six months, maybe more—Aisha couldn't wait to see what else St Urban had to offer. She just hoped her new boss didn't go into labour before they reached the old wine cellars, the next stop on their tour of St Urban.

The woman was waddling like a duck…a very pregnant, about-to-pop duck.

'How long to go?' Aisha gestured to her stomach, shortening her long stride to accommodate Ro's waddle.

Ro pulled a face. 'Eight weeks. I'm carrying twins, boys, and they are, apparently, huge.'

Aisha's eyebrows flew up. 'Seriously?'

'Seriously,' Ro replied, placing her hands on her hips and arching her back. Her stomach lifted and, underneath her tight T-shirt, Ro saw her stomach ripple. Ro placed her hand on the bump, her blue eyes soft and full of joy. 'I promised Muzi I'd start taking it easy, so I'm thrilled we managed to finalise your contract and that you are here.'

Aisha thought about the contract she'd signed and had to physically stop herself from dancing on the spot. As one of ten consultants working for Lintel & Lily, an international company dedicated to designing, decorating, renovating, and establishing boutique hotels all over the world, she'd been awarded the contract to implement Ro's ambitious vision for St Urban.

The building renovations were all done and the house stood empty. From wallpaper to the waitstaff uniforms, labourers to the layout of the gardens, it was her job to take this now structurally sound, empty building and turn it into a super-luxurious home away from home.

And if she was successful, she would be in the running for a promotion to Chief of Operations when Miles Lintel, her direct boss, became CEO when her famous and wealthy father retired at the end of the year.

The title of Chief of Operations would come

with more pressure, a huge jump in salary, and stress, but she'd finally be able to have a home base, buy a home, create her nest.

She'd been working out of hotel rooms and rented accommodation for nearly ten years, and she wanted to sleep in a bed she'd purchased, look at art she'd chosen, cook in a kitchen she'd designed.

She was tired of being a professional vagrant, a wealthy world wanderer. She'd still have to do some travelling, but she'd have her own home, roots, a city she could call hers. Established in South Africa, the now international company of Lintel & Lily had headquarters in both Johannesburg and London, and either city was an option for her home base.

Since her family—parents and four sisters—lived in Cape Town, she was probably going to choose London. She and her family tended to get along a lot better when there were ten thousand miles and a continent between them.

'Do you like the manager's cottage, Aisha?' Ro asked her, sounding a little worried.

Aisha thought of the two-bedroom cottage tucked into the trees at the back of the property with its amazing view of the toothy Simonsberg mountain. It was the beginning of autumn and the weather was still lovely, but winter was wet and cold in the Western Cape. Her cottage had a wood-burning fireplace, a cosy lounge, and a soft queen-size bed. It was beautifully, tastefully decorated and she'd be fine there.

'It's lovely, thank you,' she told Ro.

Ro's phone buzzed and she excused herself, turning away to take the call. Aisha looked around. Similar to the house, the wine cellar was a whitewashed stone building with a modest gable above its entrance, with oak barrels in a temperature-controlled, cavernous room beneath the ground floor. It was situated on the other side of a grove of oak trees, the leaves of the trees turning gold and orange. The grounds of St Urban were extensive, and a small river ran between the vineyards and the buildings. It was romantic and lovely and there were worse places to spend the next few months.

But Aisha still couldn't wait to settle into her own house, a place that was completely hers, surrounded by the things she'd spent the last ten years collecting. She'd take her time to find her perfect home, her first real home.

She couldn't believe eleven years had passed, give or take a week or two, since she'd last lived in the Cape. Over a decade since she met Pasco, ten years since their divorce. Five years since she last spoke to her parents…and she couldn't remember when last she spoke to three of her four sisters.

Like her parents, who were university professors, the Shetty sisters were all academically brilliant and unbelievably perfect. But Aisha was only on speaking terms with Priya, the only family member to stand up for her all those years ago. Priya, always the peacemaker, was overly excited about Aisha being back in the Cape and kept dropping hints about her rejoining the family flock.

'You can't be the black sheep for ever, Aisha.'

Aisha responded by telling her to hold her beer...

Being the only non-brilliant sibling, and the youngest, she'd always stood on the outside of the family circle, the one who never quite fitted in. At school, she'd been referred to as Hema's, Isha's, Priya's or Reyka's sister, and she doubted any of the teachers knew her real name. Academically average, she walked in their shadows, blinded by their light, constantly falling short of her siblings' many successes.

She'd been their sister, her parents' daughter, and then Pasco's wife. It had taken a teenage rebellion, a crap marriage, and a heartbreaking divorce, working demon hours to establish her career—basically, a long, long time—to become Aisha, and she was damned if she'd put herself in any situation that would make her question her self-worth or her place in the world.

So…no. Throwing herself back into those piranha-infested waters wasn't something she was keen to do.

'As I mentioned, we asked various landscape designers to submit their landscaping ideas and I'd like to sit down with you to discuss them,' Ro said after ending her call. She walked down the side of the building and stopped where the building ended. 'We need to get the plants in so they will be established by the time we open.'

The St Urban boutique hotel was due to open in November, a scant five and a half months away. And there was still so much to do: staff to hire and train, rooms to decorate, a marketing plan to activate. And it was her job to make St Urban picture perfect so that things ran like clockwork from the day St Urban opened its two-hundred-year-old doors to paying guests. Ro Miya-Matthews was paying L&L big bucks to make St Urban one of a handful of six-star boutique hotels in Africa.

She'd established a hotel on the edge of the Virunga National Park, in Rwanda and the Bahamas, in Goa and Bhutan. Despite her being the family dunce—her parents and sisters had genius IQs—she'd done very well for herself, thank you very much. In her eyes, not theirs.

Establishing St Urban as a boutique hotel was a challenge, but one she was more than up to.

Especially since there was the possibility of a promotion at the end of the project.

'I'm happy to look at your landscapers' plans,' Aisha replied as they resumed walking. 'Are all the building renovations done?'

Ro rocked her hand up and down. 'The tilers are just finishing up the bathroom in Suite Ten and Suite Five is being painted. The builders have told me they'll be out by the end of the week.'

Aisha was glad to hear it as she was expecting her decorating team, and the steady stream of furniture, to arrive over the next few weeks and months.

They walked around to the back of the building and Aisha immediately noticed one third of the brick wall was missing and had been replaced with floor-to-ceiling windows. She didn't recall any alterations to the cellar in the stack of documents she'd been sent.

'Ro?'

Ro turned to look at her, her stomach leading the way. 'Mmm?'

'This is new,' she stated, stepping up to the wood-and-steel structure. She cupped her hands around her face and peered into the small room through the dusty window, seeing craftsmen sanding the gorgeous yellow wood floor.

'What's going on in there?' Aisha asked her, dropping her hands.

Excitement flashed through Ro's deep blue eyes. 'Ah, that's a bit of a last-minute project.'

'What's the project?' Aisha asked, hoping whatever Ro had planned for the space wasn't too off the wall and wouldn't add numerous items to her already mammoth to-do list.

'I want a high-end, fine-dining restaurant in this space and plan on inviting exciting, interesting chefs to run the place for a limited time.'

A restaurant? For fine dining? What the hell was Ro thinking? And did she know how much work that would involve? Aisha hadn't planned to open a restaurant, for God's sake! It wasn't in the budget either.

Not that money was a problem—thanks to inheriting her biological parents' massive estate, Ro could easily add another million, or five, to the budget.

'The restaurant will accommodate up to fifteen people at a time, and I want an innovative, expensive, talk-about-it-for-ever food experience. A place that will be so exclusive, so amazing it will take months, perhaps even years to get a reservation.'

Oh, dear God. This was worse than she'd thought. One of her first solo projects was the establishment of a fine-dining restaurant in Hong

Kong and it had been a job from hell. Thanks to that nightmare, she and Miles now had an agreement: she'd work her tail off for Lintel & Lily and Miles kept her away from restaurants and picky, demanding, arrogant chefs.

The Hong-Kong-based chef had reminded her of Pasco: like her ex, he'd been arrogant, pushy, and extraordinarily self-confident.

Aisha placed her hand on her sternum, trying, as she always did, to push away the spike of hurt, the burst of resentment. Her brief marriage— nine months from the time they met to the time they separated, a year until their divorce—wasn't something she liked to think about. But St Urban was situated in Franschhoek, Pasco's home town, so she supposed it was natural thoughts of him kept crossing her mind.

Aisha didn't keep track of him; in fact, she actively avoided articles about him. But she knew he had a restaurant in Franschhoek village and spent most of his time in New York, overseeing his Michelin-starred restaurants in Manhattan.

The young sous chef she'd met in Johannesburg the year after she left school was now a household name, and a multibillionaire thanks to his restaurants, his range of food and kitchen accessories, and his wildly successful travel and cookery show. He was one of the younger, hipper and better-looking celebrity chefs and was regarded to be a rock star in the culinary world.

He'd created the life he wanted, had achieved more than he'd said he would. Aisha couldn't help wishing he'd put a fraction of his considerable energy and drive into their relationship and marriage. If he'd given her a little of the attention he'd given his career, she wouldn't have walked out on him with a sliced and diced heart. She'd thought he could fix the wounds her family inflicted, but he'd just deepened them, then poured acid into her bleeding cuts.

To find herself, to become whole, to heal, leaving him had been oh-so-necessary. Ro patted her arm. 'Miles told me you'd be fine with this, especially since you'll have help to get the restaurant off the ground.'

What type of help?

'I have someone who will give input into planning the space, and on what equipment will be needed. He's an old friend of my husband's and we trust him implicitly.'

Aisha just managed to hide her wince. Who was this guy and how much did he know about luxe dining restaurants? There was absolutely no point in spending a hundred million plus to establish a hotel for it to be let down by a less than spectacular restaurant.

Establishing an on-site restaurant was an excellent idea, in concept. She could see a tasting restaurant here…small, exclusive, lovely. But the design and the concept had to take inspiration from the hotel, as she explained to Ro.

'I understand that, I do. But my guy has a huge amount of experience and knows what he is doing.'

Aisha saw the stubborn tilt to Ro's chin and sighed. She'd come back to the subject of her consultant chef later. 'Do you have any architect plans? Have you consulted with an interior designer? One of Lintel & Lily's or anyone else?'

'No and no.'

Damn.

Aisha far preferred to work from detailed plans and briefs and she wasn't a fan of free-styling. She didn't like imposing her design preferences on a space that wasn't hers—too much could go wrong!—and chefs, in particular, were a nightmare to work with. They didn't take orders, or even suggestions, well.

What to do? How to handle this?

Aisha heard the low rumble of male voices coming from the side of the building. She watched Ro, standing at the corner of the building, turn and heard her release a long quiet sigh. Her eyes softened and her mouth curved, and a look of pure bliss crossed her face.

Aisha recognised that look, knew it well. It

was how a woman in love looked at her man; it was the way she'd looked at Pasco a lifetime ago. She'd loved him completely, as much as any woman could love her guy. She'd thought that if she made him the centre of her world, she'd become the centre of his and he'd give the love and attention she'd been missing all her life.

But Pasco's job was his first love—his only love, his mistress, and his reason to wake up every morning. She'd come, maybe, a distant fourth or fifth, or tenth, on his list of priorities.

A tall man wearing expensive chino shorts and a yellow T-shirt, a perfect foil for his dark brown skin, hurried over to Ro and laid a possessive hand on her stomach and covered her mouth with his. He pulled back and tucked a strand of Ro's hair behind her ear, his expression chiding.

'Sweetheart, you've been on your feet all day. You need to rest.'

'Don't fuss, Muzi,' Ro told him. She gestured to Aisha.

'Meet Aisha, our get-it-up-and-running manager,' Ro told her husband, pulling a face at Aisha. 'Sorry, I've forgotten your official title.'

Aisha grinned. 'Officially, I'm a hotel management consultant, but what you said works just as well,' Aisha said, shaking Muzi's massive hand. 'It's nice to meet you, Muzi.'

'And you, Aisha,' Muzi said. He looked over

her shoulder and jerked his head. 'Ah, he's done with his call.'

A tall man stepped around the corner of the house, and Aisha felt the blood drop from her head, her brain short-circuit. The world faded in and out, and Aisha heard a roar in her ears, the sound of an incoming train coming in to flatten her. This couldn't be happening to her...

It could *not* be happening.

'Aisha Shetty, meet Pasco Kildare.'

Oh, man, it was absolutely happening.

His first thought was, *There she is*, the second was that she looked amazing and the third, roaring in behind the others, was that he still wanted her.

When his brain restarted, Pasco, who'd had more practice at hiding his shock than Aisha—hers was the most expressive face he'd ever encountered—stared at her, hoping his expression remained impassive.

But, God, his ex-wife looked good. No, that was a ridiculous statement, she looked spectacular. She was tall and still slim, with a pair of legs that made his mouth water. A tangerine and white dress, her small waist highlighted by a thin leather belt, skimmed her slim frame and ended two inches above her pretty knees, the backs of which were ticklish.

Her hair was longer than it was when she was younger, pulled back from her face and hitting the middle of her back in a tumble of sable-black curls. Her triangular face was, achingly, the same. High and defined cheekbones, a full, lush mouth made for kissing and big black eyes framed by mile-long eyelashes.

He'd thought her lovely at nineteen; she was exquisite now. This stunning woman had once been his wife. He'd made promises to her, she to him, promises neither of them had been able to keep. They'd failed, he'd failed, and failure wasn't something he spoke about or advertised.

Pasco ran his hand over his face, thinking back on their impulsive decision to marry, three or so weeks after they first met. He'd needed to return to Johannesburg to start work as a sous chef under one of the country's best chefs and hadn't been able to see how, with his long hours, they'd manage a long-distance relationship. She'd told him her parents would never give permission for her to leave Cape Town, or for them to live together. Not wanting to lose her, he'd suggested they get married.

She'd surprised him by agreeing and a few days later they'd said their 'I do's in a dingy courthouse.

On a sexual and emotional high, with her reeling from a brutal fight with her parents, they'd left for Johannesburg and moved into his small flat. It had taken him less than a week to realise he was no longer responsible for just himself, he was now responsible for her: her safety, security, and well-being were in his hands. By signing that marriage certificate, he was now a husband and was under contract—in his mind at least—to provide her with stability, a home, and a decent lifestyle.

Remembering his up-and-down childhood, the famines and the feasts, he'd had a mini panic attack at the thought.

All he'd known back then was that he couldn't be like his dad, hurt Aisha the way his dad had hurt his mum. He'd known what it was like to live with uncertainty, to be scared of what tomorrow could bring, and he'd vowed, lying on their small bed in their rabbit-hutch apartment, that he'd be the husband his dad never was. He'd work as hard as he could, be successful, be a man she would be proud to call her husband. He'd show his dad, wherever the hell he was, what true success looked like. How to have it all…

In that small bed, her half lying on him, he'd vowed to give her everything. He'd never give her an excuse to leave him, a reason to walk away, leaving tornado-like devastation behind.

But, ironically, that was exactly what Aisha did.

'Hello, Aisha,' he said, rocked off his feet

when her eyes slammed into his. 'It's been a while.'

The last time he'd seen her was when he'd left for work on an early autumn morning, thinking he'd see her later, if not after the lunch service, then when he was done for the day. He clearly remembered the night before she left, how excited he'd been to tell her he'd been offered big money to take an executive chef position at a new exclusive restaurant in London. They were on their way...

He'd brought home a bottle of champagne and he'd guzzled it, telling her of his plans, how he'd use this opportunity to look for investors in his own place. She'd have to stay in South Africa for a few weeks, maybe a month or two, while she waited for her visa, but he'd find a home for them, set it up so it was ready for her when she arrived.

She'd congratulated him, they'd made love and he'd finally fallen asleep, excited about their future. This was his big chance, and he couldn't wait. Life was finally looking up.

He'd returned to an empty flat that night. Initially, he'd thought she was out with friends, a little concerned she was out so late. At midnight he'd been worried, by one a.m., he'd been frantic. At two a.m., he'd considered phoning the police. At two-ten, he'd found her note on his pillow...

The words were still printed on his brain.

Congratulations on your job offer but this isn't working and we both know it. I can't do this, us, any more. Set London on fire, Pas. A.

'Hello, Pasco.'

Muzi's sharp eyes bounced between them. 'You two know each other?'

Pasco couldn't help his cynical smile. 'We were married for about ten minutes a long time ago.'

Muzi's eyebrows lifted. 'You were *married*? Seriously? And why the hell didn't I know?'

Pasco looked at Aisha, who was rocking from foot to foot. At Aisha's insistence, he'd waited in the car while Aisha told her family she'd married him and then left the house, lugging a massive suitcase and cradling a heavy box under her free arm, her brown-black eyes wide with anguish. Her parents hadn't taken the news well, she'd told him, and she didn't know if she'd ever be welcomed back into their house.

They'd planned to visit his parents the same day, but Aisha, upset and emotional, hadn't been up to it and they'd left Cape Town without telling anyone else about their court marriage. Not wanting to break the news over the phone, he'd thought he'd tell his folks when they made one of their trips to Johannesburg, but for some reason they never made a trip that winter. Thinking they'd tell his friends and family when they returned to Cape Town at Christmas—maybe even have a church ceremony and a wedding reception—he never imagined that by September they would be separated, and divorced by Christmas.

Before Pasco could answer Muzi, Ro walked over to Aisha and placed her hand on her shoulder. 'I am sorry, I had no idea you and Pasco were married—' Ro tossed him a hot glare '—and this must be a bit of a shock for you. Let's meet again in a day or two and we can talk about the restaurant, his involvement, and you two working together then.'

He was about to speak when Aisha held up her hand. Her skin was paler than her normal shade of light golden brown, her eyes as hard as a chunk of coal. 'I'm sorry, I've lost you. What do you mean?'

Ro wrinkled her nose and gestured to the renovations. 'You're going to be working with Pasco to get the restaurant up to world-class standards,' Ro told her, looking uncomfortable. 'He's my chef consultant.'

Aisha briefly closed her eyes, and Pasco counted to ten, waiting for her to lose her cool. Aisha was fundamentally unable to step back and look at a situation through an unemotional lens.

'Whether or not Pasco and I were married has absolutely no bearing on my ability to do my job.

I am one of the best and most experienced consultants in the company and a quick relationship so long ago will not affect me in the least.'

Both Muzi and Ro released a relieved sigh, and Pasco scratched his neck, surprised at her unemotional response. He couldn't help admiring the way she pushed back her shoulders and straightened her spine. She'd grown up, he thought, become more resilient. But a *quick* relationship? God. Her words pissed him off and he felt like a fly she'd brushed off her sleeve.

'I'm a professional and I'll deal,' she told them. 'On the scale of disasters, this doesn't even blip on my radar.'

Good for her, but he couldn't work with someone who made his heart race, his mouth dry, and who'd derailed his life. He wasn't scared of hard work, relished a challenge, but expecting him to work with his ex-wife—the woman who walked out on him—was asking him for more than he could give. She'd disrupted his life once and he'd never give her, or any other girl, the power to do that again.

But she wasn't a girl any more, she was a woman. In every sense of the word.

A very sexy, very remote, incredibly beautiful woman.

And he still wanted her with a desperation he

could taste. One that scared him senseless. Another good reason for them not to work together.

'I'm so glad to hear that, Aisha. Thank you,' Ro said, smiling.

Muzi wrapped his arm around Ro's thick waist. 'If you don't need Ro for anything else, Aisha, I'm going to take my wife home,' Muzi said. When Ro didn't complain, Pasco knew she was more tired than she let on. Or maybe they were trying to give him and Aisha some time alone. Who the hell knew?

His temper was simmering, and it wouldn't take much to ignite. He wasn't ready to be alone with Aisha or anyone, so he gestured to the path that would take them back to the hotel. 'Let's all head that way,' he suggested, his words a few degrees below freezing.

Ro sent him a tentative smile. 'Actually, I'd appreciate it if you could show Aisha the restaurant space, tell her what we are thinking,' Ro said. 'That would help me, Pas.'

Pasco turned to look in the direction of his car, wondering how long it would take him to reach it. He wanted to slide behind the wheel, crank the ignition, and rocket away. He didn't need the complication of revisiting the past, wasn't keen to dredge up old memories. To re-examine the past.

Ro waddled over to him—there was no other

word for it—stood on her tiptoes and placed a kiss on his cheek. 'Thank you, I appreciate it.'

What? He hadn't said he would!

Ro told Aisha she'd touch base with her later and linked her fingers with Muzi. Pasco watched them go and, when they were out of hearing range, turned to look at Aisha again. Best to make things clear, here and now.

'This is my town, my friends, my part of the world. I'm not interested in working with you and I'm sure your company can replace you without too much trouble,' he said, his voice hard.

It took a few seconds for his words to sink in and, when they did, her eyes flashed and her nostrils flared.

'My job, my career, and I'm not going anywhere,' Aisha told him, her words coated with frustration and annoyance. 'You leave and I'll hire another restaurant consultant. I know more than a few and I don't need you.'

Yeah, she'd made that abundantly clear when she left him. Pasco gripped the bridge of his nose with his thumb and index finger, trying to banish the headache that strolled in and settled down. 'Ro is my friend and she asked me to consult on her restaurant, but I can't work with you. If you need me to, I'll talk to your boss. Give me his number.'

Her mouth dropped open and her eyes glittered with fury. 'You arrogant ass! Who do you think you are? I do not need you to talk to my boss because I'm not going anywhere. And my boss is a woman, you patronising jerk!'

'I just meant…' Why was he explaining? Goddammit! 'I need you to leave, Aisha. Just go.'

'You go!' Aisha whipped back, her temper turning her cheeks rosy. 'I'd rather be bitten by a Cape Cobra than work with you. You're the superstar chef, the one with various fingers in various pies. St Urban is my only pie, so leave it alone!

'I signed a contract, and this job is important to me, crucial to my career,' Aisha told him. She drilled a finger into his chest, so close he could see the subtle shades of colour in her black-brown irises, the tiny scar on the top of her lip. She'd changed her scent and now wore something sharp and sexy, head-spinning. Thoughts of restaurants and hotels receded and memories of her lithe and lovely body, naked of course, flashed behind his eyes. It took every shred of willpower he possessed not to lower his head, to cover her mouth with his, to drag her into his arms.

And if he did that, he might find himself on the receiving end of her right hook. She might look like the older version of the girl he married, but she'd grown up, become tougher, harder, more of a warrior.

He didn't know whether to be furious or fascinated.

Oblivious to where his mind wandered, Aisha shoved her hand into her thick hair and seared him with a hot look. 'I am staying here, and I will do my job, and that includes establishing this restaurant. If you decide to be a part of the process, you will treat me with courtesy and respect. Are we clear?'

When he didn't respond other than to raise his eyebrows, she threw her hands in the air and spun away.

She took a couple of steps before stopping to toss a furious look over her shoulder. 'I have work to do, Kildare, and you are wasting my time.'

CHAPTER TWO

LATER THAT MORNING and back in her office at St Urban, Aisha stepped out of her heels and walked across one of the two Persian carpets in her office towards the bank of windows looking out onto the extensive vineyards. In summer they would be lush and green and in winter they'd looked like little old men resting their arms on wire strands. Right now the leaves were turning and falling, creating little pops of autumnal colour across the lands. Aisha knew Muzi's company, Clos du Cadieux, rented the vineyards from Ro and she recalled reading about a rare, old country wine cultivar Muzi discovered on this property. St Urban, the property passed down to Ro by her infamous biological mother, Gia Tempest-Vane, was where Ro and Muzi fell in love.

It was a beautiful building, and the renovations to the centuries-old house were sensitively undertaken. When she brought the original handcrafted furniture back in, after having the pieces restored and French-polished, and replaced the cleaned paintings, the property would start coming to life. She could see it so clearly: luxury furnishings, amazing art, discreet staff on hand to fulfil the biggest or smallest wish, classical music piping through the common areas of the house, and the beautiful views of the vineyards and mountains enticing the guests to kick back and relax. She could make this place one of the favourite bolt-holes of the rich, famous, and stressed.

She just had to ignore Pasco Kildare while she created magic.

Aisha ran her hands up and down her arms, unable to stop thinking about Pasco. Man, he looked wonderful: sexy and strong. Ten years and a little maturity looked good on him. And just like that, she recalled his clever, mobile mouth on hers, the way he kissed. His large, skilled hands on her skin, how he could make her tremble with just one hot look. It had been so long ago, but it seemed like yesterday. She could still smell the scent of their small apartment when he cooked spaghetti bolognese, the rumble of their tired air conditioner, and the sound of taxis hooting at the crack of dawn.

Memories of their brief marriage bombarded her: their small apartment and the double bed they shared, the small desk tucked into the corner of the living room. Mismatched cutlery and crockery, the old, battered two-seater leather couch he'd found at a yard sale. The smell of his skin and the way his arms held her tight when they slept. He always groaned, then sighed when he slid into her always-willing body. He'd greet her, whether they'd been apart ten minutes or ten hours, by placing his hand on her lower back, pulling her into him—her shirt wrapped around his fist—as he plundered her mouth. He always kissed her as if he was never going to see her again and Aisha now wondered if he'd subconsciously known they would never last.

He'd been in love with his career and she'd been in love with the idea of being married, of being Pasco's wife. At nineteen, lonely, insecure, and looking for attention, she'd desperately wanted to be at the centre of the family she and Pasco created, to walk through life with a teammate, someone who had her back, someone who made her the centre of his world.

She'd met him in a pub, immediately entranced by his innate confidence. He was the guy all the men wanted to be and whom all the girls wanted to be with. She hadn't expected him to notice her, never mind spend the rest of the evening talking to her. He was a chef, he'd told her that night, but wanted his own restaurant, then a bunch of them.

She'd smiled at his ambition, liking the fact he knew where he was going and how he was going to get there. It took her a month to realise Pasco's journey required fourteen-to sixteen-hour days, and another six months to acknowledge he was a workaholic and he had no intention of slowing down, not even for her.

Maybe things wouldn't have been as bad if lack of time was their only problem, but she'd never been an equal partner in their marriage. Pasco didn't play well in that particular sandbox. He refused to relinquish any control over anything. From finances to the future, Pasco had it all planned, and her input was either ignored or dismissed. And when she did push a point, he distracted her with sex or told her he was tired and didn't want to fight, promising to make time for them to talk. He seldom, if ever, did.

It took a while, but she eventually realised they were driving Pasco's car on Pasco's highway and she was just along for the ride.

After a few dismal months of isolation and loneliness, interspersed with stunning sex, she finally realised she'd left one gilded cage to fly into another.

She'd been a needy, neglected, unseen teenager. And then she became a needy, neglected, unseen wife…

A bird flew close to the window and Aisha jumped at the sudden movement. She'd been lost in the past and she couldn't afford to let that happen. She had to live in the world as it was, not how she wished it to be.

And that meant working with Pasco to establish Ro's vision of a space to host fine-dining, pop-up restaurants. Ro was her client and keeping her client happy was how she was going to impress her boss and the board, and it was her path to promotion. Chief of Operations was as far as she could climb up the ladder of the family-owned business, and she'd be second in command. She could live with that.

For now. Aisha recalled Pasco's demand for her to leave St Urban and snorted. His arrogance was breathtaking. But Pasco had never been shy to state what he wanted; his needs and desires were paramount. Ten years ago, his career took precedence over everything else, and she was expected to fall into line with his plans.

That wasn't going to happen. She would not adjust her plans, change her course simply because he wanted her to, because he demanded it. She'd been raised in a passive-aggressive household—outright conflict was something the Shetty family avoided at all costs—but the subtle war of words, snide put-downs and coated-with-sugar insults had been just as brutal. In her years away from her family, and Pasco, she'd learned to be direct, say no, to push back and stand her ground.

She didn't like confrontation, but neither did she avoid it.

Pasco wasn't going to be able to manipulate her, manoeuvre her, distract her. She'd grown up, thank God.

Aisha tapped her lip with her index finger. This St Urban project was going to be trickier than most because the players in the game were all connected. Ro was married to the most influential winemaker in the country, someone who had an international reputation for excellence, and he was a close friend of the Tempest-Vane brothers. They were the billionaire owners of various companies, including The Vane Hotel, one of the best in the world. They'd used Lintel & Lily's services before and were regarded as especially important clients.

And Muzi's best friend was an internally acclaimed chef. And her ex-husband. Why was life punishing her like this?

Oh, and while she was questioning the universe, why couldn't Pasco have lost his hair, got flabby and pasty? It was so damn unfair he was more attractive than he'd been as a young man.

At twenty-four he'd been rangy, a little thin, but some time in the last decade he'd packed on the muscle. His shoulders were definitely broader, his thighs thicker, his arms bigger and, yeah, sexier. The man worked out, that much was obvious, hard, and often. His light brown hair was sun-streaked, and he'd taken to wearing a couple of days' growth on his lower face. Aisha wasn't a fan of stubble, but Pasco's scruff looked good on him.

His eyes, a deep, dark green and framed by short, dark stubby lashes, were as penetrating as ever. He was a harder, hotter version of his younger self and her body, dumb thing, wanted to get naked and roll around with him.

She was not going to be that stupid, she told herself. She would not jeopardise her career, her promotion, her dream for a man. She would never allow herself to be an afterthought, and she would put herself first. It had taken her years to become a confident and independent woman, and she'd never allow herself to be needy or insecure—unseen!—again.

If they were going to work together, and it was looking as if they were, they were going to have to decide on some rules. The first of which would be that she couldn't fall for him again…

Number two would be for her to be an equal

partner in the decision-making process, something she hadn't been in their marriage.

Rules would give them boundaries, a box to work within, structure...

The trick would be to get Pasco, not a fan of being told what to do, to buy into the concept.

La Fontaine was Pasco's second home and he adored Mimi, the woman who'd adopted Muzi when he was a kid, but, hell, he'd rather pull off his toenails with pliers than attend one of Mimi's famous cocktail parties. But he'd promised her he would, and Pasco wasn't one to break his promises.

Eight hours after running into his ex-wife, he parked his McLaren Artura—a gift from himself to himself—between a vintage Beetle and a classic Rolls, and rested his forehead on his steering wheel, fighting the urge to reverse and head back home. Or to go back to St Urban, find Aisha, and kiss her senseless. And then take her to bed.

He had to stop thinking about her; if he didn't, he might go completely off his rocker. He didn't want to be here, and neither was he in the mood to talk to his friends.

He most certainly didn't want to smile and be the charming, successful billionaire restaurateur with a bunch of Michelin stars under his belt, the chef with the reputation for innovative food and the pursuit of perfection.

People looked at his life and thought it was wonderful, and it was, but, damn, they didn't know what he'd sacrificed to be this successful, to attain his wealth...

They didn't know he sometimes wondered— mostly in the early hours of the morning when he couldn't sleep—whether it was all worth it.

A couple of years ago, Luka, his first mentor, passed away and Pasco flew home to attend his funeral service. He remembered his daughter's eulogy, surprised to hear that Luka had questioned whether his long hours spent at the restaurant were worth it, whether he'd make the same sacrifices again to pursue his ambitions. His words hit home and Pasco started to think something was amiss in his own life. When he returned to Manhattan, the feeling grew stronger. He was no longer happy in the fast-paced city, his creativity was stunted, and he was going through the motions, stuck personally and professionally.

He thought that maybe it was time to pare back, slow down, try something else. Believing he might be burned out—so many years of working his ass off in the industry would do that to one—and sick of New York City, he'd sold his extremely successful and famous restaurant in Manhattan, expecting to feel better.

He hadn't.

After taking a month off, bored as hell—deeply concerned he was living off his capital and wasn't earning money—he started to regret selling Pasco's, Manhattan. When Digby Tempest-Vane suggested he establish a fine-dining restaurant at The Vane, he jumped at the opportunity. Not content, he then launched a kitchen accessory line. Thinking he wanted to travel, he agreed to a six-part series to explore cooking cultures of the world and he'd thought visiting new places like Mongolia, Morocco and Réunion would make him feel whole.

It hadn't. He had everything he wanted, but he still felt as though something was missing; something hovered just out of his reach.

Maybe he was the type of guy who would never be fulfilled, who constantly needed a new challenge to keep moving forward. Having a goal and working towards it was what he'd been doing since he was a kid, desperate to be the exact opposite of his completely useless father.

They looked exactly alike, and Pasco was often referred to as his dad's mini-me. He was an almost carbon copy of him and Pasco hated it.

His father was why he was so driven, so desperate to prove himself, utterly determined to ensure he never placed the people he loved in a situation even remotely similar to the one Gerald had put them in.

With their doctor mother, and stay-at-home dad, they were seen to be a stable, solidly middle-to-upper-class family, but few people saw past the facade his dad showed to the world.

At some point in his childhood, Gerald decided to re-enter the workforce. But it wasn't in his father to take a job, and to stick and to stay. No, he wanted immediate and quick success, a shedload of money in the bank as fast as he could get it.

And because he was impatient and impulsive, he reached for every shiny object that passed him by, latched on to anyone who could provide him with the opportunity to make a quick buck. If there was a get-rich-quick scheme out there, Gerald tried it, always using his wife's salary to fund it. He also opened up numerous credit cards in her name, maxed them out, and then remortgaged their house. They lurched from crisis to crisis and Pasco remembered living with low-grade anxiety as a kid, constantly worried the sky would fall in.

As Pasco hit puberty, Gerald became increasingly desperate and massively irrational… And then everything fell apart.

Pasco pushed the memories away and rubbed

his face, the back of his neck. His father had been good for one thing, he reminded himself. Every time he looked in the mirror he was reminded of what he didn't want to be.

He'd vowed he'd never be poor, that he'd create a life of complete stability for everyone he loved. That he'd work hard for every cent he earned and he'd stay out of debt. His houses were all paid for, so were his cars, he had no credit-card debt. He had business debt, but it was manageable, under control.

Control was of paramount importance to him, and he did not trust anyone else to make decisions about his life or business.

He'd learned from his own and his father's mistakes, and he'd never, ever repeat them. Failure was not an option.

Marriage? Tried that and failed. He'd fallen in love with Aisha and after her parents freaked out about their marriage—she was too young, it was too soon, she needed to finish her studies first!—he'd vowed to protect her. Everything he did, every decision he made, was to ensure she had a stable life, that she was financially secure, and would have a husband she could be proud of.

But, after hearing about his fantastic promotion, she'd thrown all his hard work into his face and killed their marriage with a three-line note.

He'd thought they'd be together for ever, but his instincts and judgement were flawed. Trust someone again, trust his instincts when it came to love? Not a chance in hell. As for working with Aisha? Well, when hell froze over. Muzi and Ro had pots of money, and, as Aisha had suggested, they could hire a new chef consultant, it didn't need to be him. He and Aisha had had no contact for ten years so it would be easy to avoid each other for the next six months.

Pasco jumped at the thump on his car window and whipped his head around to see Muzi's face staring at him through the glass. Sighing, he hit the button for the electric window and waited for it to descend. 'What?' he demanded, scowling at his oldest friend.

Muzi placed both his hands on the sill of the car and stared down at Pasco. 'How did it go with Aisha? Everything sorted?'

That would be a hard no. 'Not yet,' Pasco replied.

'Hell of a thing, running into your ex-wife… the wife you kept from your closest friends and, I presume, from your family.'

Pasco heard the bitterness in Muzi's voice and winced. He pushed his hand through his hair, knowing he owed Muzi and the rest of his friends an apology. 'Her parents reacted badly to our news, so we decided to keep it to ourselves for a while. We knew we'd catch flak for being impulsive, for marrying so young, be questioned about whether we'd done the right thing. It wasn't something I wanted to disclose over the phone and that year was hectic for all of us, and we never made it back to the Cape. By Christmas we were divorced, I was living in London and I just wanted to put it behind me.'

'And did you?' Muzi asked.

He'd thought he had, but on seeing her again, hot and inconvenient attraction had come rushing back in, bold and bright. Aisha, then and now, affected him in ways no other woman managed to. And he didn't bloody like it.

Muzi stood up and ran his hand over his face, still looking irritated. 'You and I don't keep stuff from each other, Kildare. That being said…

'Look, I get seeing Aisha again is not ideal, but Ro needs both of you to get the restaurant up and running. She's stressed, overworking herself. Her blood pressure is up, and the doctors and I are trying to get her to slow down, to relax. She won't do that if she thinks you and Aisha are at odds, if she has to find a new executive chef or a new consultant to get St Urban up and running,' Muzi added, his words coated with a layer of worry. 'It sounds like Aisha is going to stick and stay. I need you to do the same.'

Uh…crap. 'I know of at least three chefs who would jump at the chance to be involved in a pop-up restaurant at St Urban.' Pasco machine-gunned his words.

Muzi bent down again and narrowed his eyes, his lips curling into a feral snarl. 'Do not even go there, Kildare. You promised my wife your help and involvement and she's counting on you. *I'm* counting on you. I'm already pissed off with you for not telling me you were married. Do not compound it by letting my pregnant-with-twins, stressed-out wife down.'

Ah…dammit. Muzi knew exactly what buttons to push. He started his car and sent Muzi a sour look. 'Tell Mimi I'm sorry, that something came up.'

Muzi grinned and tapped the roof of his car. 'Will do. Tell Aisha it was nice meeting her earlier.'

Yep, Muzi knew what buttons to push. Pasco's father had let him down a hundred times in a hundred different ways and Muzi knew he'd never do that to the people he loved. And that was the only reason he was heading back to St Urban to talk to Aisha, to figure out a way for them to work together.

Returning to St Urban had nothing to do with him wanting to see her again, to let his eyes feast on her, to feel the pounding in his head, and groin. It had nothing to do with wanting to inhale her gorgeous scent, to discover all the ways she'd changed and the ways she hadn't.

Nothing at all.

CHAPTER THREE

FURIOUS WITH PASCO, and emotionally and physically exhausted, Aisha decided to leave St Urban and head into Cape Town, thinking that sharing a pizza with Priya would be more fun than spending the night in her new cottage and brooding.

After changing into jeans and a lightweight jersey, she tossed her jacket onto the passenger seat and pulled on her seat belt before plugging Priya's address into her GPS. Although she and her third oldest sister talked often, she hadn't seen her in real life for over five years. It was hard to meet when one of you bounced around the world and the other had two small children, a husband, and a busy career as one of the city's best paediatricians.

She and Priya had always had a strong bond and Priya was the one who had knocked her other sisters back in line when she thought their teasing went too far. Priya had never given her Christmas gifts designed to *fix* her—self-help

books, literary classics, or gym memberships—
and had never called her the loser sibling as her
other sisters often had. She was the one who
Aisha had called when she'd needed a ride home
during her rebellious phase, who had loaned her
money when her parents had punished her by
withholding her allowance, the only person who
hadn't made her feel like a complete fool when
she'd asked for help understanding compound
fractions.

After the huge family fallout five years ago,
Priya was all the family she had.

It would be good to catch up, play with the
kids, to get to know her husband, Oscar, a bit
better. To feel as if she wasn't completely alone
in the world…

Aisha started her car, pulled away, and started
down the tree-lined driveway. As she approached
the bridge crossing over the small river, she saw
the lights of another car approaching her and
frowned. St Urban was private property—no one
else was supposed to be on the grounds, so who
was this person, and what did he want?

A little nervous, Aisha stopped and locked the
doors to her car. She watched as the car stopped
on the other side of the bridge and killed its
lights. She watched as the car door opened upwards—fancy!—and sighed when she recog-

nised the long-limbed figure climbing out of the vehicle.

Kildare.

Exactly the person she didn't want to see. Aisha pushed her head into the headrest and sighed again. She knew she couldn't avoid Pasco for ever, but she'd hoped for a little more time to get her head straight, her raging emotions under control. Nobody, before or since, had affected her the way Pasco did. He made her incredibly angry and sad, and horny and hot and frustrated…

Pasco stopped in the middle of the bridge, his hands in the pockets of his trousers, and stared at her, his expression unreadable. He wore black trousers, trendy trainers, and a soft-looking sweater the colour of thick clotted cream. The sleeves of the sweater were pushed up his strong, muscular forearms. He was strong and sexy and looked oh-so-unhappy to see her.

There was a time when his eyes warmed when he laid eyes on her, when his standard greeting was a no-holds-barred kiss, before gifting her with an I'm-so-damn-happy-to-see-you smile.

That was then, this was now.

He'd come halfway across the bridge and his actions suggested she needed to meet him there.

All she'd wanted to do was to go to her sister's place, eat pizza, drink wine and chill, catch up. She did not want to go another round with Pasco Kildare.

But she couldn't go forward—his car was blocking the road—and she couldn't retreat because she didn't want him to think she was avoiding him. Her only option was to leave the car and talk to the damn man.

She'd far prefer to drop a concrete block on her foot.

Sighing, Aisha picked up her jacket and left the car. The sun was setting, the temperature was dropping so she pulled on her leather jacket and wandered over to where he stood.

'Things are dire when you have to block the road to get a girl to talk to you, Kildare,' she told him.

'Don't flatter yourself. I was coming, you were leaving, and we can talk here as easily as we can at St Urban.'

Typical Pasco, she thought. The time and place suited him, but it didn't suit her. 'I'm actually on my way to meet someone so can we talk some other time?' She turned to walk back to her car. Pasco needed to learn the days of her rolling over at his command were long over.

'Got a date?'

A frisson of excitement ran up her spine at the hint of jealousy in his deep voice, and Aisha fought the urge to spin around. After counting to ten, then to twenty, she slowly turned and looked up into his moss-green, forest-deep eyes.

'Yes,' she lied without hesitation or a smidgeon of guilt.

Pasco's jaw hardened and his lips flattened. 'Tough.' An owl hooted and he turned his head towards the sound, his eyes scanning the trees.

'I've decided to help set up the restaurant and am considering Ro's offer to be the guest chef for three months when it opens. I'll send you an email as soon as possible concerning the kitchen equipment specs, what decor I want, the layout.'

Again, he was making assumptions without her input, just as he used to do when they were married. 'That's not going to work for me,' she told him, lifting her chin.

'Why not?' Pasco demanded.

'I'm not your lackey and I don't take orders from you. Secondly, I don't *want* to work with you,' she told him. 'I'm going to convince Ro to find another chef to consult on the restaurant.'

Pasco's frustration-filled eyes collided with hers. 'You will do no such thing.'

'Newsflash, you're not the boss of me.' Really, who did he think he was trying to boss her around? His sous chef? One of his waitstaff? Arrogant jerk!

'Ro is stressed and being stressed isn't good for her or the twins. When she hears we can't work together she'll worry and then Muzi will rip off my head.'

'I don't really care what happens to your head,' Aisha told Pasco.

'But you do care what happens to Ro,' Pasco quickly responded.

Dammit, he had her there. Though she'd only just met her, she liked Ro and she didn't want any harm coming to her or her babies.

'Look, I want to work with you even less than you want to work with me, but Muzi is my best friend and Ro means a lot to me. I try not to disappoint the people I love.'

His words were an arrow straight through her heart. 'Except that you had no problem hurting me!'

As soon as the words left her mouth, she wished she could pull them back. She sounded every inch the wronged and bitter wife. Dammit, she shouldn't be feeling anything for him, not after such a short relationship so long ago!

'Hey, you were the one who left me!' Pasco told her, his voice rising.

'And it was so easy for you to let me go!' Aisha retorted.

What was it about this man that made her temper bubble, her tongue fly? Her childhood home was a shouting-free zone—her professor parents preached dialogue and discussion—and she never lost her temper at work, but Pasco managed to blow every one of her fuses. How was she going to be able to work with him if all they did was shout and/or snipe at each other?

Aisha folded her arms against the chill of the autumn night and looked up at the swathe of stars above her head. It was a beautiful night, and she was in the company of a beautiful man, but one who despised her.

She couldn't blame him for that—she did walk out on him without warning, leaving him a note explaining nothing. If he'd done that to her, she would still be angry too.

At the time she'd known that if she'd tried to explain her thoughts and feelings, explain that he didn't *see* her, that she needed time with him, he'd either kiss, charm, or persuade her into staying. She'd tried to talk to him, but he always deflected the conversation or distracted her before she managed to convey the depths of her unhappiness. And on the rare occasions she had managed to get her point across, he'd made no effort to give her the time she'd so desperately needed.

Talking and staying was a habit, and she'd broken that cycle with a note and by actually leaving.

The past was the past and nothing could be changed. But she could get a handle on what was happening now. Especially since the stakes were so damn high. If she did a good job at St Urban, she'd get a promotion. If she didn't, she wouldn't, and she'd stay where she was, spending months and months in strange countries. Another shot at promotion wouldn't come any time soon, if it came at all.

Just calm down, Shetty...and think!

Ro is your client, and she wants Pasco to work with you. You can't ask her to choose between the two of you because, if you did, you'd probably lose. Pasco is her husband's best friend and it seems Ro and Pasco genuinely like each other.

If you want to work at St Urban, then you have to work with Mr Annoying. Also known as Mr Annoyingly Sexy.

Shaking off the thought, Aisha decided she had to treat Pasco as she would any other consultant.

But with stricter rules.

'We need to establish some goalposts, guidelines...' God, what was she trying to say? 'We need to work out the rules.'

'Rules?' Pasco asked, his expression derisive.

Aisha dropped her hand to nail him with a hard look. 'Yes, I know, you are a hotshot chef who doesn't think rules apply to him, but with our history and if we are going to be working together, then we need some.'

'There's only one rule...' Pasco told her, hands

on his hips. 'Do what I want, when I want it, and we'll get along fine.'

Had he changed at all? If she had to judge by that comment, then he hadn't, not even a smidgen. Aisha clenched her fists, her fingernails digging into her palms. She hoped he was teasing her, but in case he wasn't she couldn't back down, be seen to be weak. If she did, Pasco would gobble her up and spit her out. Not happening. 'You really should see somebody to talk about your delusions of grandeur, Kildare.'

She saw a gleam in his eyes she didn't like but decided to ignore it. 'That tongue of yours has got sharper, Aisha Kildare—'

'Aisha Shetty. I dropped your name as soon as I could.'

Pasco responded with a mocking smile. He slid his hands into the pockets of his trousers and raised his dark eyebrows. 'Why did you come back here, Aisha?'

'What do you mean?' Aisha asked him, confused by the swift change of subject.

'Did you do some research, find out that I am good friends with the Miya-Matthewses and apply for the job to establish St Urban to edge your way back into my life?'

Aisha snorted, amused. But then she realised he was being heart-attack serious. Seriously?

'Why on earth would I be interested in doing that?' she demanded, her tone terse.

'Ten years ago, you left me because I was a poor sous chef, and couldn't give you the life you wanted, the life I promised you, but I'm not poor any more. And I have contacts within the hospitality industry that would be valuable to you, people like the Tempest-Vanes, and other hoteliers all over the world. Hooking back up with me would be a smart move.'

Did he really believe she left him because they lived in a tiny flat and because money was tight? How could he think that? She would've lived in a tin shack with him, anywhere in the world, if he'd given her a little attention, some of his time. She opened her mouth but yanked the explanation back. The statute of clarifications had run out a long time ago.

'So, I'm back for your cash and your contacts,' Aisha mused. 'Interesting.'

Seriously? Could he be any more arrogant if he tried? She didn't think so.

Aisha felt the long roll of annoyance, the slow, acidic burn of anger. But because she knew disdain was far more effective than screaming, she sent him a below-zero smile full, she hoped, of pity. 'Yes, of course, I'm here because of you. And only you. My being here has absolutely nothing to do with the fact I am Lintel & Lily's best consultant, on track to be the youngest chief of operations ever appointed. Obviously, my studying my butt off to get my MBA and the years I spent in the field gaining experience in establishing hotels all over the world was all because I have this decade-long master plan of returning to the Cape and sliding back into your life!'

She patted his arm, happy to see his eyes widen in surprise. 'You're so clever for working that out, Kildare. How on earth did I manage to live this long without you and your asinine opinions?'

If he responded with a sarcastic comment, she'd kick him in the shins with the pointy end of her sexy shoes. She held her breath, waiting for his reaction. She expected either a blistering retort or maybe, if unicorns existed, a subdued and quiet apology...

What she did not expect was him to take two quick steps to reach her, standing so close Aisha could feel the heat of his body, see the faint scar bisecting his right eyebrow, a tiny birthmark on his right temple. His car lights fell on his face and his stubble held shades of brown and blond and his eyes were a deep, dark mysterious green, the colour of kelp beds off the Atlantic coast. She could see the passion in his eyes and felt her own bubbling inside. A part of her wanted to turn and run, but her feet were glued to the ground, her body demanding to know his again. She needed to taste him again, to run her hands through his hair, across his broad shoulders.

She shouldn't be feeling this transfixed, so fiercely attracted, but she was. Dammit.

He opened his mouth to speak, but instead of forming words, his mouth covered hers in a hot, frustrated, kill-me-now kiss. She tried to remain unaffected, told her body to stay statue-still, but after ten seconds, maybe twenty, she sank against him, her defences crumbling under his skilled mouth.

He tasted like whisky, felt like home. His tongue twisted around hers and she was back in their apartment, nineteen again and in love, desperate for his hands to skim her body, his mouth to explore her skin. Her hands danced across his back, skimmed over the dip of his spine. She sighed at the hard layer of muscle under his clothes, the softness of his hair as it slid through her fingers.

God, the man could kiss, a heady combination of confidence and competence, desire, and a hint of desperation. Nobody, before or after, came close to the way he made her feel...all loose and lazy yet hyped and heady.

She loved what he did and hated the way he made her feel.

Aisha put her hands on his chest and pushed

him away, desperate for some distance between them. He was too attractive, too magnetic, and, despite his being an utter ass a few minutes ago, she wanted him.

So, nothing much had changed in more than a decade, then.

Dammit.

She lifted her head, saw triumph and pure male satisfaction blazing in his eyes. 'You still want me,' he stated, sounding more than a little cocky.

The arrogant, presumptuous, conceited ass! She opened her mouth to blast him and saw him lift one, just one, supercilious eyebrow. He was expecting her to lose her temper, was goading her to do exactly that. He wanted her to be a shrew, to throw a slap, to lose her temper…to make a fool of herself.

She was damned if she would give him the satisfaction.

Right, one of them had to be the adult and she'd drawn the short straw. She straightened her spine and pushed back her shoulders.

When their eyes connected, she folded her arms across her chest and tipped her head to the side. 'I've always known you are a determined, driven guy who likes getting your way, but to-night you've been the absolute worst version of yourself. I hope that's an aberration and not who you are now. But understand this, Pasco…

'You were talking nonsense earlier and you know it!' She waited for a beat, making sure she had his full attention. 'Hear me clearly, Kildare. Nothing you can do or say will stop me from working with Ro, from establishing St Urban as one of the best boutique hotels in the world. And if Ro wants a tasting restaurant on the premises, that's what she will get, with or without your co-operation. We had a very unequal relationship in the past, but I'm not the same meek, mild, and easily led girl I was before. Do not be in any doubt about this…if you bite, I will bite back.'

By the end of her soliloquy, she was shaking, and Aisha hoped Pasco was too mad to notice. Gathering her wits, and her pride, she turned around and headed back to her car, slid behind the wheel, and slammed the door shut. Without looking at him, she executed a quick three-point turn and drove back up the road to St Urban.

Nothing to see here, folks. She'd only kissed, argued with, and lectured the only man she'd ever loved, the man she'd once promised to share her life with.

It had been, by anyone's standards, a hell of a day.

Pasco owed Aisha an apology, a huge one.

He'd been way out of line last night and he felt like an utter ass. She'd been right to call him out and her cool lines, delivered so disdainfully, had cut through all his BS.

He had been arrogant in his dealings with her, and the high point of his idiocy had been suggesting she'd returned to the Cape to be with him. Even more annoying was his small wish that it were true.

Pasco, dressed in his oldest pair of jeans, and his most comfortable boots, walked up the road towards St Urban, looking up at the branches of the oak trees forming a leafy canopy over the road. The trees were flaunting their beautiful colours, red and gold, and bronze, and now and again one drifted down to the road, dancing on the light breeze. His property, a smallholding he'd bought on selling his restaurant in New York, had once been part of St Urban and bordered Ro's place to the east. His house wasn't far from her new abode, the manager's cottage situated in the corner of the property. Instead of walking for a good forty-five minutes, he could've hopped a couple of fences, crossed a paddock, navigated his way through a vineyard, and reached her place in ten minutes.

But the long walk had given him time to think and, God, he knew he needed every moment to work out how he could apologise without sounding like a complete moron.

On returning to his place last night, he'd

headed straight for his home office and fired up his state-of-the-art laptop. He'd never, not once, done an Internet search on Aisha in all the years they'd been divorced. He didn't believe in looking back, or torturing himself, so he'd kept his curiosity tightly leashed. He'd initially typed 'Aisha Kildare' into the search engine and couldn't understand why he came up with no results or, to be accurate, nothing relating to her. He realised his mistake and with a thumping heart typed in her maiden name and various images and results jumped out at him. There were testimonials about her work as a consultant—all five stars—a write-up stating she was one of the hospitality sector's most exciting and innovative consultants, and he came across a series of articles she'd written for a trade magazine. Then he visited the Lintel & Lily website and, under their 'Meet Our Team' tab, read the write-up on his ex-wife. She had, indeed, received her MBA, graduating near the top of her class. She'd set up hotels in far-flung, sometimes inhospitable places and was respected for her cool head and her practical streak. She was fast, efficient, and smart, and a valued member of the Lintel & Lily family. Her employees and clients adored her.

Basically, if someone wanted to set up a hospitality-based operation, Aisha Shetty was the person you hired to do that. Ro had employed the best of the best.

And he was, as she'd said, an ass.

An ass who needed to apologise.

Pasco pushed his sunglasses up into his hair and rubbed his tired eyes with his thumb and index finger. Sleep, always elusive, had been non-existent last night. He'd sprawled out on his couch in front of his large-screen TV, watching reruns of old international rugby games, but his full attention had been on the hot-as-fire kiss they'd shared. They'd always had chemistry, but their kiss last night had gone beyond that; they'd been radioactive. Her body, slimmer than it had been when she was younger, had fitted against his perfectly, and her scent, edgier now, had invaded his nostrils and settled in his brain. And her mouth, God, her mouth…her taste. It kicked up a yearning in him to know her again, to discover all the ways she'd changed. And the ways she'd not.

Pasco kicked a stone with his boot and watched it skitter into the grass. Taking Aisha back to bed was not a good idea, in fact, it was a comprehensively disastrous one. They'd tried once, they'd failed. He wasn't into reliving the past, revisiting mistakes. So, no, jumping back into bed with his ex was not a good idea. But he still wanted her, goddammit.

Impulsively, Pasco veered left and ambled down the path leading to the cellars. He walked around to the back of the building to look at the renovations for Ro's restaurant. He slipped through the unlocked door and, standing on the newly sanded floor, looked at the unpainted walls and the magnificent view.

This…

A restaurant like this was his unspoken, deepest, never-spoken-of dream. A small kitchen, doing most things himself. Growing as much produce as he could in his own gardens and orchards, picking it in the morning and using the ingredients for lunch and supper, his entire focus on creating excellent food in a non-pressurised environment, forgetting about stars and rewards and reviews.

In a perfect world and alternate reality of himself, he'd ditch his high-pressure restaurants, his travel shows, and the persona of being the country's first international celebrity chef. He'd read, work on a cook book, wander about in a greenhouse he built, raise chickens and goats, make cheese. He wouldn't run from business to business, project to project, dealing with staff and suppliers, making sure the steep and exacting standards he set were consistently exceeded by himself and his staff.

He was tired, dammit.

But whenever he considered closing down his restaurants, leaving his high-powered life, he felt his heart rate speed up, a hand squeezing his lungs. He knew what it was like to lose everything of value, houses and cars and, yeah, money, knew how devastating it was to have his life flipped upside down in the blink of an eye. Living a simple life, free of pressure and ambition, was a lovely idea, but it was a pipe dream, a mirage.

He needed different eggs in a variety of baskets so that if one venture failed, another would keep him afloat. He needed the pressure, the accolades, the five-star reviews, and the attention because it put distance between him and his father, reminded him he was nothing like the man who was so determined to have the easy life while putting in little to no work. Growing up, all he'd heard was how like his father he was, that they looked the same, talked the same.

He might be his father's mini-me, but working hard, moving fast was his way of showing the world that, below the surface, he wasn't his father's son.

He had pots of money but one bad decision, one financial misstep, could wipe a business out. That was why he had backup plans for his backup plans, ten different slush funds, and why he diversified. If something went wrong with Pasco's at The Vane, he could rely on income from Pasco's, Franschhoek and his share in Binta. If they all went belly up, he could expand his travel and cooking show. He would not be like his mother and be blindsided.

No, stepping back, having a small restaurant, pottering really, was a nutty dream. And he was anything but daft. He'd satisfy those cravings for a small restaurant by helping Ro set up hers and, possibly, running it for a month or two. That would have to be enough.

Pasco left the cellar and headed for the path that would take him to the manager's cottage, conscious of the spark of excitement burning in his belly. Since he seldom felt excited about much any more, he reluctantly admitted he was eager to spend more time with his ex-wife. His all-grown-up, now feisty, occasionally fierce, ten times more attractive than she had been, kissed like she was on fire, ex-wife.

Pasco sighed. God, he was up the creek, his paddle was long gone and hungry alligators were snaking on his ass.

Excellent.

CHAPTER FOUR

ON RETURNING FROM her five-kilometre run through the pear orchard, past the stream, and through the vineyard—showing off its lovely autumn colours—Aisha jumped into the shower and afterwards pulled on a pair of black yoga pants, fluffy socks, and a comfortable, slouchy, off-the-shoulder cotton sweater. She intended to work from the cottage today and the four-seater square dining table in her open-plan lounge, dining, and kitchen area suited her perfectly. She had coffee and, because she'd stopped by a deli and bakery in Franschhoek yesterday, she had enough food to tide her over for a couple of days.

She anticipated a day of immense productivity.

But first, she wanted to take five minutes to relax. She picked up her cup of coffee and walked onto the tiny patio leading off from the kitchen and sat down on the white concrete wall enclosing the small area. There was a small wrought-iron table, but she wanted to feel the sun on her face, so she sat on the wall, back against the cottage, and stretched out her legs. The smell of lavender and thyme, planted in raku-fired pots, wafted up to her and she could hear tractor engines rumbling in the distance.

It was a perfect day, clear, cool, and sunny, and Aisha couldn't take her eyes off the Simonsberg mountain basking in the sunlight. It was like a huge dragon's tooth, raggedy edged, filled with cracks and crevasses. She'd read, somewhere, that it could be hiked, and she'd love to do that. Maybe in a month or two when she had a handle on her work here at St Urban, she'd carve out the time.

You left me because I was a poor sous chef and couldn't give you the life you wanted, the life I promised you...

Last night, after her anger had died down, Pasco's words had kept buzzing around her brain. Where and when did he pick up the notion that money, or lack of it, was the reason she'd left him? Of all the reasons she'd bailed, and there were many—lack of time and attention being the biggest reason—money had never been an issue.

She had been all but excommunicated by her parents, so her uncle Dominic had stepped up and paid for online university modules and, when she could, she'd picked up waitressing shifts at the bistro down the road. They hadn't been rich, but they'd been a long way off poor.

'Stunning, isn't it?'

She wasn't surprised to see him, had even expected him to turn up this morning as he wasn't one to leave an argument unfinished. What did surprise her were the battered, faded jeans hugging his hips, and old, mud-splattered boots. The cuffs on his long-sleeved T-shirt—navy blue and hugging his wide, wide chest—also showed some signs of wear and tear.

But the watch on his thick wrist was a limited edition Patek-Philippe, his sleek and sexy aviator sunglasses were high-end, definitely designer. She couldn't name the brand, but knew they'd be ferociously expensive to buy. His hair was expertly cut and his cologne, dancing on the light breeze, was a compelling mixture reminding her of the sun and the sea, and a blend that perfect cost money. Lots of it.

He looked fit, hot, and take-me-to-bed sexy, but Aisha had no intention of letting him off the hook. He needed to do some big-time grovelling first. 'What do you want, Kildare?'

His eyes deepened and desire flashed, briefly, in his eyes. Yeah, yeah, she got it, he wanted her, their kiss last night clued her in, but if those were the first words out of his mouth she might throw her coffee cup at him.

Pasco jammed his hands into the front pockets of his Levi's, those huge shoulders rolling forward. 'To apologise, actually. I was off base last night. I was pissed off and frustrated and I should never have said what I said.

'You're obviously damn good at your job and I was way out of line,' he added. 'I'm sorry.'

Aisha, shocked at his sincere apology—the Pasco she knew would rather burn Wagyu beef than apologise—needed a minute to think, so she lifted her coffee cup to her lips and sipped, trying to formulate a response. She'd been expecting another fight—Pasco hated losing—but she hadn't expected an apology.

This was new. And she could either accept it and move on or take the opportunity to needle him a little for his assumptions. *Be an adult, Shetty.*

Aisha nodded. 'Thank you.' She saw him looking at her coffee cup and sighed. 'Do you want a cup?'

'I'd love a cup,' he replied, stepping onto the patio. Aisha swung her legs off the wall and walked into her kitchen, Pasco a step behind. She grabbed a mug and put it under the spout of the coffee machine and checked the level of the beans and water.

'I didn't hear a car, so how did you get here?' Aisha asked him.

'I walked over,' Pasco replied, pulling out a chair. He lifted his eyes at the piles of multicoloured folders on the table and cocked his head to read the tabs. 'I own the smallholding right next door, actually. This cottage is about a ten-minute walk, as the crow flies, from my back door. But I took a long way around and walked up St Urban's drive.'

Aisha turned her back to him, not sure how comfortable she was with him living in such close proximity to her.

Pasco pulled out a dining chair and sat down. 'Franschhoek is my home town so I bought a place here.'

'It's a long commute to Pasco's at The Vane every day,' Aisha said, placing his mug in front of him. It was black and strong, the way he used to drink it back in the day.

He picked up the pottery mug, sipped, and closed his eyes. The corners of his mouth kicked up. 'I see you still drink Ethiopian Yirgacheffe.'

She smiled and shrugged. Money had been short during their marriage but some things, Pasco had declared, could not be compromised on. Coffee, excellent South African wine, exceptional olive oil. 'Some famous chef introduced me to it and got me hooked. I had severe withdrawal symptoms because I couldn't afford it on my student budget, but as soon as I started earning decent money, it went back on the list.'

'That chef taught you well.'

He had. She'd learned a lot from Pasco about food and wine and making love. Aisha, feeling her cheeks redden, remembered his comment from last night and decided to take the plunge. 'Talking about money, you said something last night that shocked me.'

Pasco winced. 'Only one thing?'

She smiled briefly. 'I don't want to fight with you this morning, I don't.' She lifted a finger. 'And we really do have to work out the rules of our working together, Pasco.'

He waved her suggestion away. 'Later. What did I say to shock you?'

'You said I left because you didn't earn enough money, because you didn't give me the life I wanted.'

Pasco nodded. 'I didn't.'

Aisha held his hard stare, needing him to believe what she was about to say next. 'I never left because we were financially strapped, Pasco. That was never a problem. Other things were, but not that.'

'What—?'

'No, that's enough for now,' she interrupted him. She nodded to the window and the awesome view of the sun shining on the mountain.

'It's a beautiful day and I'm declaring a truce. Please?' Not giving him a chance to argue, she switched subjects. 'We were talking about your commute to the city.'

Pasco didn't drop his eyes from hers and she knew he was digesting her words, trying to make sense of them. She caught the impatience in his eyes and knew he wanted to dig, needed more of an explanation. She hoped he didn't push; she really wasn't up for another fight.

Pasco dropped his eyes and when his shoulders dropped, Aisha knew she was safe. For now.

'At some point, we'll pick up where we left off...'

Of that she had no doubt. Just not this morning, thank God. 'I don't live here permanently, I just use my Franschhoek house as a bolt-hole,' he continued. 'I have an apartment in Fresnaye, but my chef de cuisine, or executive chef, runs the restaurant on a day-to-day basis.'

'Nice gig if you can get it,' Aisha said, sitting down opposite him.

'Hey, I've worked long hours for a long time to earn that sort of freedom,' Pasco snapped back.

Wow, his work ethic was a hot-button topic for him. And, yeah, she knew exactly how hard he worked as she'd been the one waiting for him at home.

Aisha cast around for a neutral topic of discussion, but Pasco beat her to it by tapping on a folder. 'Tell me about St Urban.'

That was an unexpected question. 'I'm sure Ro told you all about her plans for the place.'

Pasco tucked his long legs under the table and his knee brushed hers and Aisha felt the familiar tingle, the hit of connection. Pasco folded his forearms on the table and shook his head. 'I haven't had many discussions about St Urban with her. We've all, Muzi, Ro, and I, been so busy with our respective projects—St Urban, Muzi launching a new wine from a rare cultivar he found on the property and my launching a range of cooking accessories and foodstuffs— that when we do get together the last thing we discuss is work.'

Pasco's wicked grin flashed. 'Honestly, all we've discussed lately is Ro's pregnancy.' He pulled a face. 'I know more about pregnancy and birth plans and multiple births than I need to, thank you very much.'

Aisha smiled. 'It's pretty exciting they are having twins.'

'It's pretty scary because they are having twin boys,' Pasco corrected her. 'I knew Muzi as a kid and he was wild!'

Aisha raised one eyebrow. 'And you weren't?' She pretended to think. 'Weren't you the guy who drove his car through the window of an art gallery in town?'

'You remember me telling you that?' Pasco asked.

She remembered everything he told her about his teenage years, boarding school, and his adventures with Muzi and Digby Tempest-Vane. But he never spoke about his childhood before he came to live in this valley in his early teens. Then again, she never spoke about her family either.

'St Urban, Aisha?' Pasco prompted her.

'Right.' Where to start? She glanced at the folders, wondering where to begin. 'Okay, let's start with the manor house. It was important to Ro, from the beginning, to preserve the elegance and grandeur of the house, so distinctive details like the hand-painted dado rails and the broad yellow wood floor beams, and a million others, have been kept and, if needed, restored. After extensive renovations, the manor house can now sleep sixteen, with six en suite bedrooms and a family suite. She's also converted the smaller guest house and the venue can sleep eight. So we have space to host over twenty people in supreme luxury.'

'Uh-huh,' Pasco murmured. Aisha wiggled in her seat. She'd forgotten what it was like to have all that intense energy and attention focused on her. When Pasco listened, he concentrated. And she knew that, in a week, a month, or a year, he would be able to recite their conversation verbatim.

Unfortunately for their marriage, he'd only paid attention when he'd wanted to, when the subject had interested him enough. Her unhappiness hadn't.

Oh, maybe that was unfair. The truth was more nuanced than that. In hindsight, she thought Pasco hated talking about their problems because then he'd have to admit there was a problem, that there was something he—they—couldn't instantly fix. Unlike cooking, you couldn't toss your wife out and start from scratch.

Anyhoo...

'I'd like the guests to feel like they stepped into their second home so, while everything must be exquisite, it must also feel welcoming. Ro and my boss, Miles, who is currently Chief of Operations for Lintel & Lily, felt the same way and that's the direction they went in. The library will be full of books, the lounges will have plump couches, and there will be fresh flowers everywhere. Luckily, the house was filled with antique furniture when Ro inherited so a lot of the desks, tables, dining tables, and bedposts will go back into their original rooms when they have been restored and polished.

'I'm planning luxury picnics by the river, hiking and mountain-biking trails, a small bar stocking the best liquor money can buy. The guests will be able to drink cocktails on the veranda or under the massive oak tree with the wide spreading branches. Damn, I need a mixologist.' Aisha picked up her phone, opened a document, and tapped in a note to look into whether the budget would support a mixologist.

'Talk dirty to me, Aisha,' Pasco murmured.

Her eyes flew up and connected with his. 'What?' she asked, blushing.

He grinned, and Aisha felt as if she were touching the sun. 'Talk food. Chefs, produce suppliers, menus.'

She leaned back and crossed her legs. 'For the manor house kitchen, I'm thinking farm to table, seasonal, local, lovely. That's all I have, right now. The rest depends on who we hire to run the hotel kitchen.'

'Do you have anyone in mind?' Pasco asked her, running his finger up and down the edge of his coffee cup.

'No, not yet. I'll advertise the position in a month or two, and if I don't find someone suitable I'll work through a recruiting agency.'

'I have one or two ideas on supremely talented people who would jump at a chance to run their own kitchen and who'd be up for the challenge. I can get their résumés to you.'

'Thank you, I'd appreciate it. Muzi is restoring the cellars and he wants to install a winemaker here. He's going to focus on producing wine from the rare cultivar he found. Muzi will also be employing the staff needed for wine tastings and cellar tours. The cellar is so old and such an amazing space and I'd like to find a historian who can give me a history lesson of winemaking in the valley and, hopefully, of St Urban itself.'

'My brother Cam is a winemaker and he's the area's local-history nerd. I'm sure he could give you what you need.'

Aisha made another note on her phone. 'You are proving to be surprisingly helpful this morning, Kildare.'

'Glad to be of service,' Pasco replied, amused. 'Right, let's get down to business… Ro's pop-up restaurant. Where are you with that?'

Aisha looked at him and spread her hands. 'Nowhere because that wasn't something I was aware of until I got here yesterday.'

Pasco pushed back his chair, extended his long legs, and crossed his feet at the ankles. He looked relaxed, yet Aisha knew that under that lazy-looking exterior was a mind running at a sprinter's pace and never stopped.

'The tasting-menu restaurant has been low on her list of priorities. It was an idea we chatted about a little after she and Muzi got together, but never really pursued. Then she fell pregnant and it slipped even further down the list. But a couple of months ago, I told her that I was interested in doing it, but only for a few months. She liked the idea of bringing in different world-class chefs on a rotating schedule.'

So that was how the idea of a restaurant was born. Good to know. 'So why are you getting involved in designing the restaurant?'

'Because I'm good at it and have a rep for sky-high standards when it comes to decor, service and, obviously, the food itself. I like to have, at the very least, input into the design of the restaurant and complete control over the food, the menu and whom I work with.'

'All that and without you putting a cent of your own money into the project,' Aisha said, impressed by his cool confidence and a little frustrated by his arrogance.

Pasco's green eyes slammed into hers. 'I am one of the best chefs in the world and people will book into St Urban just to eat my food.'

Aisha cocked her head and sent him a look from under her lashes. 'You really need to work on your self-confidence and self-worth, Pasco.'

He picked up a pen from the table and threw it at her. 'Cheeky brat.'

Aisha looked out of her kitchen window to the sunlight falling on the mountain and nibbled on the inside of her cheek. 'I'm going to be the point person representing Ro on the project, Pas. Are we going to be able to work together?'

Pasco's expression remained steady and imperturbable. 'Why wouldn't we?'

Oh, let me count the ways.

'Because you are demanding and bossy and determined to have your way. And so am I,' Aisha responded. 'I'm not the person I was before, Pasco.'

'I would be disappointed if you were, Aisha. People are supposed to grow, you know.'

He wasn't getting what she was trying to say. 'But I'm not just going to nod my head and say, "yes, Pasco", "no, Pasco", "three bags full, Pasco". I'm going to argue with you, contradict you, flat out tell you no, occasionally.'

He stared at her, the corners of his mouth twitching. 'I'm becoming more terrified by the moment.'

God, he wasn't taking her seriously. She reached across the table and poked her finger into his biceps. 'You aren't listening to me, Kildare! My loyalty is to Ro and her vision for St Urban. If you want or do something contrary to that vision, I'm going to put my foot down.'

'I know that you will try,' Pasco told her, still smiling. 'Relax, Aisha, we'll find our way.'

She knew that he meant that she'd come

around to his way of thinking. Insufferable man! She poked him again. 'Don't say I didn't warn you, Pasco.'

He looked down at the finger barely denting his skin. 'Is that supposed to make an impression?'

She yanked her hand away and scowled at him. He grinned, pushed to his feet, and glanced at his watch. 'Where are you going?' she demanded. 'We still have things to discuss!'

He looked from her to the coffee cup in his hand. 'I was just going to make myself another cup of coffee.'

'Oh,' Aisha replied on an internal wince. 'You could've asked me first!'

'Honey, we've been married and divorced, and I got you hooked on this particular drug, so I thought we were beyond that. Do you want a cup?'

'No, yes, okay.' Aisha speared her hands into her hair and sucked in a deep breath. Twenty minutes in and she was already exhausted. She'd forgotten that dealing with Kildare was like trying to wrestle an octopus. And, off subject, the way those Levi's cupped his butt was enough to make angels drool.

He turned, caught her ogling him and lifted an eyebrow. Aisha blushed, annoyed by his grin and the satisfaction in his eyes.

Yeah, he was a good-looking guy and she wasn't immune. She wouldn't touch, that would be stupid, but she could look. A little. A very little.

'Rules of engagement...' she muttered.

Pasco resumed his seat. 'What are you muttering about?'

Aisha waved her index finger between them. 'We need rules. Last night I tried to talk to you about how we were going to work together and we got distracted.'

'That's one way of putting it,' Pasco drawled.

She ignored his comment and pulled a writing pad towards her. Picking up a pen, she clicked the top a few times before jotting down a few bullet points.

He craned his head to look at her writing and released a frustrated huff. 'Your writing is revolting.'

'Yours, I recall, isn't much better,' Aisha retorted. 'I'm making a note of what we need to discuss...things like the budget, decor ideas, equipment, staff. Oh, and we need a name.'

'Pasco's at St Urban,' Pasco whipped back.

'Uh...'

'I have Pasco's at The Vane, Pasco At Home— that's my brand of kitchen items and food-stuffs—Pasco's, Franschhoek. The name is part of my brand, instant name recognition, and that's what this restaurant, if I sign the contract, will be called,' Pasco said, determination in his eyes.

Aisha wrinkled her nose, knowing she'd already lost this battle. Luckily, she saw the reasoning behind his words and was prepared to hand him this victory.

'Okay, then, let's talk about how and when we're going to meet.' She pulled her tablet towards her and opened her calendar. She turned it to face him and gestured to the mostly blank squares. 'As you can see, I'm pretty free, but that will change shortly. So, pick a date. I think we should meet a couple of times a week.'

Pasco shook his head. 'That's not going to work for me. My schedule changes from day to day. I go where I'm needed, do what I need to do as the day unfolds. The best I can do is give you a couple of hours' notice when I'll be free.'

Aisha felt her jaw drop, not sure she was processing his words correctly. Was he seriously suggesting she build her calendar around him? Did he not realise how much she had to do, the mountain of work ahead of her to get St Urban up to standard? She was already operating under time constraints and that was before she heard about the pop-up restaurant.

But now, like then, Pasco's work came first. Aisha felt the wave of resentment and looked away so that he didn't see how much his blithe words affected her. So, nothing had changed, not really.

And how sad was that?

She could say something—she should say something—but honestly, she was tired and didn't have the energy to fight. Aisha scratched her forehead, worried she was slipping into the patterns of the past, allowing Pasco to walk all over her again.

'I see some things haven't changed.'

He frowned, trying to work out what she meant. Dammit! She hated it when passive-aggressive comments slipped out—she was better than that.

She held up her hand. 'No, that won't work for me. You need to give me definite times when we can meet because I am not sitting around waiting for you to call.'

She waited for his response and wondered if she imagined the flare of respect she saw in his eyes. Probably. Pasco took their empty coffee cups to the sink and when he returned to stand in front of her, he slid his hands into the back pockets of his jeans and nodded. 'Fair enough. I'll see what I can do, but I'm slammed.'

'Make time, Pasco, this is important.'

'Noted.' He darted a look at his watch and sighed. 'Talking of, I need to get to The Vane.

I have a meeting and then we are spending the afternoon testing new dishes.'

Naturally, Sundays were never a day of rest for the workaholic chef. Aisha looked at her dining table and sighed. Rocks and glass houses, baby.

At the doorway, Pasco turned to face her and lowered his head, as if aiming for another kiss, or to brush his lips across her cheekbone or forehead. He hesitated and she saw awareness flash in his eyes, a reminder to both of them that what they had before, what was acceptable back then, might not be welcome now.

They had to rewrite the rules, find new ones, toss others. Tiptoe through this minefield.

Keep it simple and, for goodness' sake, keep it professional. She sent him her most impersonal smile. Or at least she hoped she did. 'I'll see you around, Kildare.'

'Don't be like me and work all day, Aisha.' Yep, there was that hint of bossiness she remembered so well.

'Like you, I don't have time to relax, Pasco. I have a million things to do and minimal time to get everything done. That's why I need your cooperation.'

'I'll try my best, Aish.' His eyes met hers and his expression turned rueful. 'I know that I can sound autocratic, but I understand what burnout feels like, Aisha, and I'd hate it to happen to you.

So do as I say and not as I do and take some time off to relax.' Instead of dropping a kiss on her temple or on her cheek, he squeezed her shoulder. 'I'll let you know when we can meet again.'

Aisha watched, annoyingly tingly and turned on, as he walked out of her back door. Taking, she noticed, the short route back to his house.

CHAPTER FIVE

ON FRIDAY MORNING, Pasco skirted the back of St Urban's manor house and headed for the old carriage house, which Ro had converted into offices for the hotel manager and the admin staff. Walking inside, he heard voices coming from the end office, wandered down the short hallway, and leaned his shoulder into the frame of the door to watch Aisha pacing the floor of her messy office, her hands on her hips and her back rigid.

'Yes, I understand I have to get the order in today to take advantage of the old pricing structure, but I need to get my consultant to sign off on the order and I can't get an answer from the man!'

That man would be him. Pasco winced. His bad.

He'd had about a dozen emails from Aisha over the past fourteen days and nearly as many phone calls, all of which he'd ignored. Not because he didn't want to talk to her, but because he was worried that once he started down that pitted-with-peril path, he wouldn't be able to find his way back. As it was, he spent far too much time thinking about his stunning, sexy ex-wife.

In between lurid thoughts of what she looked like naked—gorgeous, of that he had no doubt—and imagining what he would do to her if he ever got the chance to see her like that again, he rolled her words over and over in his brain, trying to make sense of what she'd said.

'I never left because we were financially strapped, Pasco. That was never a problem. Other things were, but not that.'

If money hadn't been the problem, then what else had caused her to run? He wanted to know, but also didn't. Their time had passed and there was no point in looking back, but he hated the idea of getting something so important wrong.

He did recall stumbling in after a long shift and seeing her sitting on their sofa, her hands under her thighs and her eyes reflecting trepidation and determination. He'd quickly learned her I-need-to-talk expression and that was, after a busy, high-stress night, the last thing he'd wanted to do. Make love to her, sure, he was always up for that, but talking? Not his thing.

Maybe that was one of their problems: he'd been eager to gloss over their problems and pretend everything was fine. It hadn't been fine. A quick marriage, an even quicker divorce, and years of not communicating proved that theory. Talking about his feelings, *anyone's* feelings, made him feel scratchy, as if he were standing in a leaking bucket on a storm-tossed ocean. Unsure and vulnerable…he hated exposing himself emotionally.

Idiot that he was back then, he'd always assumed she was going to whine that they never had any fun, but fun required money and time, and they were barely keeping their heads above water.

Whenever he saw her I-need-to-talk face, he made it a game to see how long it would take him to distract her, to move her off the subject. Luckily for him, she was putty in his hands and one deep kiss and a thumb across her nipple normally distracted her…

God, he'd been a jerk. Young, arrogant, full of himself.

He was now paying the price for his youthful arrogance because he couldn't stop thinking about the real reason for her unhappiness and needed to know what had made her run. He burned with curiosity and his inquisitiveness annoyed him. He and Aisha were done, nothing remained…

Except his need to make love to her, with her,

again. That hadn't gone away. If anything, it was bigger and bolder than before.

Crap.

And, yes, this was difficult to admit, but the more time he spent with her, the urge to be with her grew stronger. He didn't have the time to devote to a significant other—

God!

She was his ex-wife, someone he worked with, why was he attaching the words *significant* and *other* to thoughts of her? He was not getting involved with her again.

Bottom line, he couldn't afford to spend great swathes of time with her, wouldn't give her that much importance in his life.

They. Were. Done.

The only reason he was here, in her office, was because he was on his way to Pasco's, Franschhoek and it was a quick detour to St Urban. And also because the tone of her messages and emails had changed from polite and professional to increasingly irate and he suspected he was dancing on her last nerve. He couldn't be around her without wanting to kiss her senseless, but neither did he want to alienate her.

Aisha Shetty still had the ability to flip his world on its head.

Fifteen minutes… He'd give her fifteen minutes and then he was out of here. He could keep his hands off her for that long, surely?

When the call disconnected, Aisha looked up at the ceiling and released a low, intense scream, her arms linked behind her head.

'Problem?' Pasco asked when her arms dropped.

She whirled around, heat in her cheeks and fire in her eyes. He'd never seen her look so beautiful. 'What the hell are you doing here, Kildare?'

Pasco's eyes dropped to her wide mouth, remembering the feel of those sexy lips under his. 'I thought I saw at least two dozen emails from you demanding that I drop in. This is me, dropping in.'

Aisha pursed her lips and Pasco was pretty sure she was counting to ten. Or maybe, judging by the seconds ticking by, to twenty. 'I have been trying to get hold of you for the past two weeks,' Aisha stated, pushing the words out through gritted teeth.

'I've been busy,' Pasco told her, walking into the room. God, a temper looked good on her, her eyes flashing brown-black fire and her skin rosy with frustration. He jammed his hands in his pockets to keep from reaching for her and hauling her into his arms and slowly stripping her so that he could see her standing naked in the sunlight pouring into the room.

'You are an intensely frustrating man, Kildare,' Aisha told him, pushing her hair back with both her hands.

'So I've been told,' Pasco replied, keeping his tone easy and his hands in his pockets.

He sat down on the hunter-green tufted leather camelback sofa he presumed came from the manor house. He stretched out his legs and crossed his ankles.

'I have fifteen minutes. Talk.'

Aisha looked at him as if he'd grown six misshapen heads. 'You have got to be kidding me! I need hours and hours of your time!'

'Fifteen minutes is what you are getting.' He glanced at his watch and mock-grimaced. 'Thirteen now.'

Aisha's hand curled around the stapler and he hoped she wasn't going to throw it at his head. Her lips moved in what he was sure was a curse and he relaxed a fraction when she released her grip on the heavy-duty stapler. Glaring at him, she reached for her tablet and tapped it, her luscious lips flat with annoyance.

'That was the supplier of the commercial refrigerators. The prices are set to rise and if we want delivery at the old prices, we have to place an order immediately.'

Pasco forced himself to concentrate. He'd recently come across a new supplier with advanced technology, and he wanted to explore that option. 'I'm still investigating other options.'

Aisha rested her butt on the edge of her desk—wide, old, a bit battered—and glowered at him. She wore a navy jumpsuit teamed with a sunshine-yellow jacket, but the happy colour was totally at odds with her scowling face. 'I gave you this information ten days ago, Kildare!'

He grinned at her growly voice. 'And I'm working on it. Next?'

Hand on stapler again. If he got out of here without stitches, he'd call himself fortunate. 'I received a portfolio containing sketches of the interior decor. We need to decide on a look, especially if you want custom-made furniture and a custom-made bar.'

Fair point. He nodded. 'I'll take the portfolio when I leave, and I promise I'll give you feedback by the end of the week.'

Aisha didn't look convinced, and he honestly couldn't blame her. 'You do know that today is Friday, right? That today is the end of the week?'

'Technically, the end of the week is on Sunday.'

His pithy comment resulted in a low, sexy growl. He hadn't set out to annoy Aisha, but he enjoyed her in-his-face exasperation. She'd been a lot more accommodating as his wife and, if he was being honest here, a bit of a pushover.

Grown-up Aisha was tough, feisty and he was as mentally attracted to her as he was physically.

That wasn't good news.

Pasco stood up, walked over to her and stopped a foot from her, briefly closing his eyes as her lovely scent hit his nostrils. He wanted to bury his nose in her neck, between her breasts, to get a full hit of her perfume.

Liar—he wanted far more than just to smell her scent.

Pasco plucked her tablet from her grasp and looked down at her neatly typed, bulleted list on the screen. There were still fifteen or so items they still needed to discuss and, dammit, he'd never be able to do justice to her list in a couple of minutes. She was right, she needed hours and hours of his time. He couldn't afford to give it to her, not when he was holding on to his control by the thinnest of strands.

'Email me this document,' he instructed her, wincing at his rough voice.

'I have! Numerous times!' Aisha retorted, eyes flashing. 'Pasco, you are making this a hundred times more difficult than it has to be. I've set up a fine-dining restaurant before—just step back and let me handle it. You don't have the time, don't seem that interested in it—'

'God. You are lovely.'

She blinked, unsure she'd heard him correctly. 'What?'

He wasn't quite sure where the words, so totally unrelated to their conversation, came from, but they couldn't be contained. Because, God, she was. Gorgeous, that was. With her eyes flashing with irritation and her pursed mouth, she was the embodiment of a warrior princess.

'Your skin is flawless and your scent drives me insane,' Pasco muttered.

Surprise flashed in her eyes, along with a hint of pleasure. 'Thank you, but we were talking about...'

Her words faded away, and all he could think about was that he had to have her mouth under his, his hands on her soft, warm, fragrant skin. He saw desire in her eyes, watched her mouth part, and her tongue darted out to touch her bottom lip. It was obvious she'd lost her train of thought and he was glad he wasn't the only one descending into madness. Aisha sighed, took a step closer to him and it was all the encouragement he needed. He dipped his head slowly, giving her enough time to pull back, and then his lips met hers.

He'd thought he wanted hot and fast, sexy and strong, but he surprised himself by gentling his kiss, skimming his lips across hers in a barely there movement. He felt Aisha tense and he waited for her response, fully expecting her to push him away. But instead of her hands slapping his chest, her mouth softened, her sigh hit his lips and she lifted her hand to curl her fingers around the back of her neck. She stood up on her tiptoes to push her mouth against his, sliding her tongue into his mouth.

Yes…*this*.

Their tongues tangled, his hands skimmed over her back, her butt, her ribcage. This kiss was strange, sweet, tender, so powerful in its simplicity. A man and a woman who wanted each other, the soft torment of tongues colliding, hands stroking… What was more basic than that?

Basic and mind-shatteringly powerful.

They were just a man and a woman who wanted each other, Pasco reassured himself. They'd always had explosive chemistry…it didn't mean anything. It couldn't. But, just in case it did, in case he deepened the kiss and took her on that couch—he was so damn tempted—Pasco lifted his mouth off hers and rested his forehead on hers.

'Where's the portfolio, Aisha?'

Aisha dropped her hands from his neck and stepped back, confusion replacing the lust in her eyes. Pity. But necessary.

She pushed her hair off her face and sucked in a deep breath. 'What?'

'The interior decorator's portfolio of sketches that you want me to look at?' It took everything he had to sound professional, businesslike. How the hell his brain was functioning sans blood, he had no damn idea.

'Uh—' Aisha glanced at her desk, still trying to gather her thoughts.

He spied a large leather portfolio on the credenza behind her desk and stepping away from her took a considerable amount of effort. He picked up the portfolio and held it up. 'This it?'

'Yes,' Aisha replied. She folded her arms and rocked on her feet. She glanced at his mouth, shook her head and straightened her shoulders. Her cool expression told him she was taking her cue from him and was happy to pretend that nothing had happened between them, that they hadn't shared a kiss that had rocked his world. 'But I need to explain—'

Hell, no. He needed to get out of here before he lost the battle to take her on that couch in the middle of the day. Not that he had any problem with midday lovemaking— *Crap, Kildare! Pull it together!*

'I've set up a lot more restaurants than you have. I'll figure it out.' He made a show of looking at his watch. 'Time is up, I've got to go.'

'But—'

Pasco didn't dare look at her again—didn't need to, he could hear the anger in that one word—and swiftly walked to the door. He jerked the door closed behind him and, two seconds later, heard the sound of that heavy stapler crashing against the wooden door.

Yep, not unexpected. And probably deserved.

Aisha stood in the doorway of a closed health shop and eyed the busy entrance of Binta, a famous oceanfront venue a seagull's cry away from one of Camps Bay's most famous beaches. Every Capetonian and most South Africans had heard of the iconic oceanside spot, a cornerstone of the city's social scene. It was laid-back, vibey, expensive, and casual and on any other day she'd be happy to meet Priya for a drink and a meal as they watched the magnificent sunset.

But, unfortunately for her, Priya was hosting a party for her husband's fiftieth birthday in Binta's private dining area and most of the extended Shetty family would be in attendance.

Marvellous.

She'd tried to get out of attending, tried very damn hard. But Priya had shot down her every excuse. It was Saturday evening so she shouldn't be working anyway, and she was staying in Priya's guest suite so she wouldn't have to worry about driving back to Franschhoek—or any-where since her sister lived in a massive house just down the road and she'd walked to Binta. Priya had also received reassurances from the rest of the family that they'd leave the past in the past.

Hah. They'd try, but Aisha was expecting more than a few snide comments. She assumed there would be a lot of wistful wishing—*We all wish Aisha followed her sisters into the sciences, but it wasn't to be*—and the backhanded compli-ments that always made her want to run scream-ing from the room. Five years ago, her parents were finally on the point of forgiving her for her disastrous marriage when events, more accu-rately her sister Reyka, conspired to hurtle them back into stony silence.

She'd video-called her folks every month or so for the past two years, brief, light conversations, but this party would be the first time she'd see her parents in the flesh for more than a decade and she was as nervous as hell.

Damn Priya for insisting on her being here. Yes, she understood she couldn't avoid them for ever, that she'd have to see and speak to Hema and Isha, and deal with Reyka, but she didn't want to. It would be much easier to go back to St Urban and work. She had so much to do, a hotel to get off the ground, and she didn't need the drama her family always rained down on her head. She always came away from encounters with them questioning herself and the path she'd chosen; feeling less than, and irritable for feeling that way.

Aisha looked across the road to the ocean and wished, for the first time in a long time, she had a masculine hand to slide hers into, a shoulder to place her head against, a strong arm around her waist. Someone to stand in her corner, someone tough and protective, who wouldn't hesitate to step in when he felt she was being bullied or disrespected. Yes, she was a strong woman—she'd learned to be one—but even strong women sometimes needed to lean, craved some support.

She'd love to have Pasco here…

There, she'd admitted it. He knew nothing about her family, except she had a bunch of sisters and that her parents didn't approve of their marriage. She'd never spoken about them, told him how she was bullied and put down, how alone and unseen she felt. Early on in their relationship, she'd realised their time together was limited, and she hadn't wanted to spend the rare moments they had discussing her childhood.

They hadn't talked much, or at all. Aisha pushed her thumbnail between the tiny gap in her two front teeth as she watched the waves roll onto the beach. He hadn't opened up to her either... God, it was tough to admit that they knew each other's bodies inside out, but not each other's minds or hearts. What drove them or hurt them, made them happy, or what made them cry.

All they'd had was an out-of-control attraction. And it was bigger and brighter than before. She'd tried to ignore it to concentrate on business and had sent him another round of emails and left irate messages for him to get in touch—though, to be fair, he had given her feedback on the restaurant's decor and had authorised her to order some kitchen equipment—but there was still so much to do. On Monday, she intended to hunt him down again and, hopefully, they'd get through more than two bullet points this time.

But if he kissed her again—if she kissed him back—all bets, and possibly clothes, were off.

Aisha glared at Binta's pretty facade. *Just get this done, Shetty. An hour, two, and you can leave. And if you don't drink, you can drive back to Franschhoek tonight.* Gathering her courage, Aisha stepped onto the pavement, the skirt of her long-sleeved ankle-length maxi dress swishing around her ankles. She touched the thin black leather belt encircling her waist, thinking she liked the patterned fabric in white and fuchsia and the black edging at the hem and neckline. It was conservative but a little boho, a lot stylish. She'd pulled the sides of hair off her face and allowed the rest to fall down her back and kept her make-up understated. She looked good, but knew her mum and sisters would find something to criticise.

They always did.

Priya and Oscar stood just inside the door of the restaurant, looking exactly what they were: a hugely successful, beautiful couple living their best life. After Aisha received a hug from Oscar, Priya took both her hands and danced on the spot. 'Isn't this place fantastic? I can't believe we managed to book it.'

Aisha looked over her shoulder into the busy bar and lounge area and lifted her eyebrows on seeing an A-list Hollywood celebrity sitting at one of the tables. Binta was vibey and sophisticated and, judging from the laughter and buzz of conversation, looked like a fun place.

Maybe when her family got too much she could hide out down here and order one of Binta's world-famous cocktails. Something citrusy and wonderful and strong with alcohol. She'd need it, of that she had no doubt.

'Everyone is upstairs. We're just waiting on a couple of guests and then we'll join you upstairs.' Priya saw her wince and quickly added, 'Or you can wait downstairs with us.'

'I'll wait.'

Priya squeezed her hand again before turning away to greet a couple she'd never met before. Aisha stepped back, leaned against the wall, and watched as people, mostly dressed in designer clothes, streamed past them to enter the downstairs bar area. She liked the way the doors folded back, leading onto the patio area, separated from the road by huge arches. The room was also filled with luscious plants that provided the tables with some privacy but didn't impede the view of the beach and the setting sun. It looked like what it was reputed to be: a world-class, vibey joint that was the place to see and be seen.

'Oscar and Priya, I presume?'

Pasco? What the hell?

Aisha blinked, then blinked again, but it was definitely Pasco standing in front of her, dressed in a Prussian blue suit over an open-necked white shirt, brown leather belt, and shoes.

Priya placed her hand in his and smiled. 'Pasco, how nice to meet you at last. This is my husband, Oscar.'

Pasco shook Oscar's hand before tuning to Aisha. 'Hey, Aish, you look lovely.'

Aisha started to tell him he looked lovely too, but quickly shut down that thought. 'Why are you here?' she demanded.

Pasco looked around and shrugged. 'I show

up here every few weeks just to keep an eye on the place.'

'Why would you do that?' Aisha demanded.

Pasco looked from her to Priya, and her sister rolled her eyes. 'When you told me you were working with Pasco again, I called Pasco up, introduced myself as his ex-sister-in-law, and asked for recommendations on where to hold Oscar's fiftieth. He suggested Binta and designed a special menu for us,' Priya explained.

Her sister had never been shy about putting herself forward. Aisha looked at Pasco and pulled a face. His slow, heat-filled smile caused her stomach to flip inside out. 'Sorry,' she mouthed and saw his tiny shrug.

The pieces started to fall into place. 'You own this too?' she asked him as Priya and Oscar turned to greet more guests.

'With a partner,' Pasco told her. He gave her a long up-and-down look and silently whistled. 'You do look great, Aisha.'

She fought the urge to swish her skirts as a four-year-old would. Seeing the admiration and lust in his eyes made her feel warm and squishy and rather wonderful.

Then she remembered he'd spent the last week ignoring her again. 'You've been avoiding me,' she accused. 'Why?'

Pasco placed a hand on her back and led her to the stairs. 'Honestly?'

'Yes, of course,' Aisha replied, thinking how wonderful his big, warm hand felt on her lower back.

'Because every time I'm within six feet of you, I have to fight the urge to kiss you senseless… everywhere,' he said as they climbed the stairs.

What did he mean…? Oh, right. Well…um…

'I'm not sure what to say to that,' Aisha admitted after a long silence.

At the top of the stairs, Pasco stopped and looked down at her, his smile rueful. 'It'll be a bloody miracle if we manage to get this restaurant up and running, I admit that.' He gestured to the door down the hall. 'That's where you want to go.'

No, she didn't. Aisha stared at the half-open door and grimaced. 'I'll just wait for Priya and Oscar here.'

'But your family is through there. You look a lot like your mum, by the way,' Pasco said.

Aisha pulled her bottom lip between her teeth. 'Do they know you are here?'

He shook his head. 'No, I don't make a point of introducing myself to guests.' He frowned and pushed back his jacket to slide his hands into the pockets of his trousers. 'Are they still pissed about us marrying?'

'When it comes to me, they are always pissed about something,' Aisha admitted. Hearing footsteps behind them, she turned to look down the stairs and saw Priya and Oscar following another couple up the stairs.

She pulled up a smile for Pasco and lifted her index finger to drill it into his chest. 'We need to talk, to work. Why don't we meet in a very public place next week and we knock this project on its head?'

Pasco nodded, his smile wry. 'Yeah, okay.' He glanced towards the private dining room, his knuckle skimming her cheekbone. 'If you need rescuing, give me a missed call.'

'Thanks, but I'll be fine,' Aisha told him. 'I don't plan on staying more than an hour, two at the most.'

Pasco dropped a kiss on her cheek, and Aisha ignored her sister's coy whistle as he walked away. She glared at Priya, saw a million questions in her eyes, and placed her finger against Priya's ruby-red lips. 'Not one word, Priya, I mean it.'

Priya nodded, but as soon as Aisha dropped her finger, her words flew out. 'One question, just one! Why the hell did you let that gorgeous creature go?'

Reasons, Aisha silently replied. Many, many reasons.

CHAPTER SIX

PASCO STOOD JUST inside the service door leading
to the private dining room, his eyes on Aisha.
Thank God Binta's managers were brilliant at
their jobs, because he'd been less than useless
since Aisha arrived.

Nobody, before her or since, had managed to
distract him the way she did.

Pasco moved to allow a waiter carrying a tray
of sushi to pass him and immediately stepped
forward again so that he could see her clearly.
She stood in a group comprising her mother, two
of her four sisters, and two other women who
were either aunts or old family friends. Fifteen
minutes had passed since she'd joined the group
and Aisha had yet to say a word. Judging by her
carved-in-stone face and fixed smile, she'd taken
a couple of verbal hits and her body language had
changed from uncomfortable to I'm-so-over-this.

Anyone who looked closely enough could see
the misery in her eyes, her tension. It was in her

hunched shoulders and in the way she held her champagne glass in a death grip.

Unlike everyone else, Aisha wasn't having any fun...

Damn this. He couldn't stand here and watch her suffer for a minute longer. Turning around, he walked down the short passageway and stepped into the very busy kitchen. He caught the executive chef's eye. 'Do you have everything in hand?' he demanded.

'Absolutely.'

'Good man. Have you seen Jenna?' he asked, referring to the senior of the two on-duty managers. He was told she was in the storeroom and Pasco headed in that direction. She walked out of the room as he approached it, her arms full of bottles of rum.

'We're having a run on mojitos,' she cheerfully told him.

'Excellent,' he replied. He pushed a hand through his hair, feeling uncomfortable. 'Would you and Sbu be able to cope if I took off?'

She nodded. 'Sure.'

'I'll be on my phone if you need me.'

Jenna flashed him a smile. 'Boss, we often run this place on our own. We're good, I promise.'

He was micromanaging and he knew it. He loved control, having it and wielding it, and stepping back was always difficult to do. But right now, Aisha needed him and this business didn't. 'Thanks. Call me—'

'We won't,' Jenna told him as she sauntered away.

Right. Pasco pulled his phone out of his jacket pocket and pulled up Aisha's number. His fingers flew across the screen as he tapped out a message.

You're not having fun so I'm sending a waiter to you. He'll escort you to the staff car park where I'll be waiting. Do not make me come and find you because you know I will.

Aisha stepped into the small car park at the back of Binta to see Pasco lounging against his McLaren Artura, his long legs crossed at the ankles. Her eyes collided with his and she sucked in a deep breath, barely remembering to thank the waiter for showing her the way. He was such a man, Aisha thought, as she walked towards him. Confident, hyper-masculine, alpha to the core. Intelligent, good-looking and ripped, the man had it all. Could she be blamed for her many X-rated fantasies?

Tucking her clutch bag under her arm, she walked across the small car park, her eyes not leaving Pasco's as he walked around the bonnet of his car to open the passenger door for her.

'Are you okay?'

She wanted to lie but couldn't. 'Better now.'

Aisha settled herself into the passenger seat and moments later Pasco sat beside her. Being with him made her feel stronger and invigorated her. He was like her own custom-made energy drink, a one-of-a-kind battery charger. She turned her head to look at him and found him watching her. Their eyes clashed, collided, neither of them able to look away and tiny fireworks exploded on her skin. After what felt like minutes, she managed a small smile.

'Aren't you supposed to be working?' she asked.

'Honestly, that place is so well run, I feel like I'm in the way.'

'It's not like you to be hands-off,' Aisha said. In fact, she knew that Pasco never shirked his duties, ever. If he said he was going to do something, then he always followed through. Their marriage was his only failure. The thought made her sad.

'Binta doesn't need me, you do.'

Aisha's eyes widened at his statement. He was putting her before work? What was happening here? 'I was with my family,' Aisha stated, keeping her tone light. 'It wasn't like I was facing a firing squad.'

'You hated every bloody minute, Aisha. Don't

try and tell me that you didn't,' Pasco muttered, jabbing the start button on his car. The engine roared to life, and she felt its power in her feet, up her spine, deep inside her.

'I hated every minute,' Aisha conceded as he pulled out of the car park into the main road. Aisha watched as heads swivelled towards them, and she noticed the pointed fingers and appreciative gazes his fancy car elicited.

'Where are we going?' she asked, half turning to face him.

'Somewhere where we can talk.' He flashed her a smile as they crawled down the busy road. His smile could power the sun and there was nothing better than feeling it against her skin.

'Public or private?' Aisha asked. She shrugged when his head snapped around. 'C'mon, Pas, we both know that if we go somewhere private, we won't do any talking.'

Pasco turned his attention back to the road and Aisha saw the tension in his jaw. 'Public... *dammit.*'

Ten minutes later, he pulled into a parking space about five hundred metres down the road from Binta. After opening her door for her, he took her hand and led her across the busy street to a small, old-fashioned dusty-pink double-storey house. There were tables on the veranda and servers bustled around like flies on steroids.

Pasco ignored the steps leading up the veranda, steered her around the side of the house and up a flight of steel stairs. He pushed a doorbell and after a few seconds, the door clicked open.

An attractive woman dressed in a short black cocktail dress smiled at them. 'Hello, Pasco.'

'Busi.' Pasco dropped a kiss on each of her cheeks before introducing Aisha.

'Are you busy tonight?'

Busi rocked her hand up and down. 'Most of the regulars are at a cocktail party at The Vane, so no, not right now. We'll pick up later.'

Aisha looked across the mostly empty banquettes and tables to absorb the view. Needing to take it all in, she walked away from Pasco and Busi to reach the veranda, taking in the expansive vista of ocean and sky. She had an awesome view of the Lion's Head and Twelve Apostles mountains, and a stupendous view of the beach.

'This is amazing,' she told Pasco when he finally joined her, holding a whisky in one hand and a huge margarita in the other. 'What is this place?'

Pasco guided her to a comfortable two-seater couch. 'It's called The View, for obvious reasons. It's a cross between a boutique bar and a private club. You have to be a member to come here.'

'And do you own this too?'

Pasco sent her a slow smile. 'I don't. And

that's why I can relax here.' He lifted his drink and clinked it against her glass. 'Cheers.'

'Cheers.' Aisha took a huge sip of her drink and sighed when the perfect ratio of sweet and sour hit her tongue. She whimpered and wrapped both hands around her glass. 'God, you have no idea how much I need this.'

'So what's the deal with your family?'

She'd been expecting his question, had even thought up a couple of glib responses to divert him. But suddenly, she didn't want to lie or fudge, she just wanted to tell him the truth.

'My sisters are all academics, as are my parents. They are very respected scholars and lecture at the university. They are intensely, ridiculously brainy and I am not. They see success in terms of academic achievements, and I let down the side.'

'That doesn't make any sense, Aisha. You're one of the most organised, logical people I've ever encountered. And you have a master's degree.'

'In business. It's one of the most common postgraduate programmes around and nothing special. My sisters are doctors and scientists who, as my parents frequently remind me, are making a difference in people's lives. I do not.'

He stared at her, his expression intense. 'That's not all of it.'

No, it wasn't. Aisha took another sip of her drink and rested her head against the back of the couch. 'They are so passive-aggressive, Pasco, I can't deal with them. Sometimes, I just wish they'd yell and scream and get it out, but they don't, they prod and poke and whinge and whine.'

'You seem to have a good relationship with Priya.'

'I do. She never gave me copies of *Maths for Dummies* for a birthday present, or a framed photograph of my sisters all holding their PhDs. And she was the only one who took my side when…' She hesitated, not sure if she wanted to tell him about that ugly incident. No, she did want to tell him, she just wasn't sure he wanted to hear it. She and Pasco weren't good talkers. Lovers, yes. Communicators? Not so much.

'Tell me, sweetheart.'

She sipped her margarita and half turned to face him, dragging her eyes off the view. But, honestly, looking at Pasco was as good. 'After I told them that we divorced, it took a long time for them to reach out to me—well, Priya did, but no one else. Anyway, two years later the lines of communication opened up, but it was very obvious that if I was a disappointment before, I'd sunk to new lows.'

'I'm sorry.'

She shrugged and blinked away the moisture in her eyes. 'Five years ago, it was my folks' fortieth wedding anniversary and I saved up to buy them tickets to visit me in London, as well as a tour of six different cities in Europe. Four-star hotels, private tours, it cost me a freakin' fortune.'

'What happened?' Pasco gently asked, placing his big hand on her thigh. It felt right there, just as it felt right to lay her head on his shoulder.

'About a month before they were due to leave, Reyka, the sister just older than me, got engaged. And strangely, the only time she could hold the engagement party was smack in the middle of my parents' trip. I begged her to postpone it. She wanted me to rearrange my parents' trip, but I couldn't. I'd already paid for everything and to change dates was incredibly expensive. I just didn't have the extra money.'

'How long were they going to be away for?'

'A month.'

Pasco pulled back, frowning. 'She couldn't hold off on having the engagement party for a month?'

Aisha shook her head. 'Apparently not. My two eldest sisters supported her, Priya tried to support me but my parents were forced to choose.'

'And they chose an engagement party that could've been postponed,' Pasco stated. *'Wow.'*

Aisha sat up and reached for her drink. 'Tonight was the first we've been together as a family for ten years. Judging by the way they behaved, I was never married, Reyka wasn't a complete bitch and I didn't lose a whack of money.'

Pasco skimmed his hand over her hair. 'I'm so sorry.'

'It is what it is.' Aisha shrugged and tried to smile. She sat back and draped one leg over the other, leaning her shoulder into Pasco's. For the first time that day, she felt marginally relaxed.

This was a little slice of heaven and she intended to enjoy it. The margarita was cold, the fading sun still warm and a stunning view in front of her. And, for once, she wasn't surrounded by spreadsheets and lists, stressing about what to do next.

Aisha slid her feet out of her shoes and wiggled her toes, sighed deeply and tipped her head back and closed her eyes. She hadn't felt this relaxed for…

'Why did you walk out on us?'

Aisha shot up and spun around to look at him.

Pasco took a sip of his whisky and winced on seeing her shoulders shooting towards her ears. Excellent way of killing the mood, Kildare!

'Wow, that's an out-of-the-blue question. Why are you asking me now, ten, nearly eleven years later?'

Because he needed to know, now. Tonight. 'Why, Aisha? You left me with a goddamn note and nothing else.'

Shame flickered in her eyes, only to be extinguished a second later by annoyance. 'Pasco, I tried to talk to you! I told you I was unhappy, that I never saw you, that I was lonely.'

'I was working, Aisha! Trying to create a decent life for us.'

She took a deep breath, and when she spoke, her voice was calm. Well, calmer than his. 'But that's the thing, Pasco, *you* were trying to create a life for me, for us. We should've been doing it together. You made all the decisions, you plotted a future for us that I didn't have a say in, partly because I never saw you and when I did, we rarely talked. We'd make plans, but they always fell through because your work always, always came first. You never made me a priority and I felt like a visitor in your life.'

He stared at her, shocked. 'Why didn't you tell me you wanted to leave me? Why didn't you give me a chance to fix it?'

'Pas, I tried to...so many times. But you always told me you were too tired to talk, you changed the subject, or you seduced me. The few times I did get you to listen, my unhappiness never sank in because your behaviour never changed. You didn't make the effort to give me what I needed.' Aisha lifted one shoulder in a helpless shrug. 'Then you took the job in London without consulting me. It was a massive decision, we were moving to another country, but you made the call…all on your own. That was what broke me, broke us.'

He started to argue, only to realise he didn't have a decent defence. He'd done exactly that, made the decisions, planned their life, so damn sure he was doing the right thing. His motives, to provide a secure life for them, for the children he'd imagined having with her—for him to be the exact opposite of his feckless, useless father—were good.

But the execution of those plans, he reluctantly admitted, could've been better. He could've brought her into his confidence more, asked for her input on the plans he'd been making. He'd been so damn arrogant, confident and self-involved.

'I made so many mistakes with you, Aisha, and for that I'm sorry.'

Shock flashed across her face, and he didn't blame her, as apologising wasn't something he often did. Or at all. He pulled a face. 'I'm happy to take responsibility for the part I played in the destruction of our marriage.'

She gave him a shaky smile, obviously taken aback by his apology. Admittedly, so was he. But while they were on the subject, there was just one more thing he needed to say. 'But you could've at least told me that you were leaving, that you wanted a divorce. You should've told me all that to my face.'

To his surprise, Aisha nodded her agreement. 'Absolutely. That was wrong of me and I'm sorry.'

Her sincere, easy apology rocked him. God, they'd been so young and made so many mistakes: his fuelled by pride and stubbornness, hers by fear, loneliness, and insecurity. Pasco raked a hand through his hair. He caught her eye and tried to smile. 'So where do we go from here, Aish?'

Aisha placed her hand on his forearm and squeezed. 'We can't go back, Pasco, but I'd like us to be friends.'

It was pretty difficult to be her friend when all he wanted was to back her against the wall, press his body into hers and ravish her mouth. Fill his hands with her lovely breasts, her mouth with his tongue. He wanted her to wrap her long legs around his hips, wanted to hear her breathy moan as he slipped inside her heat, capture the sound of his name on her tongue as she flew apart.

Yeah, friends. Much easier said than done.

They watched the sunset and an hour rolled into two, then three as they caught up on the last ten years, silently agreeing to skirt topics touching on their marriage and divorce. He told her about his businesses, about living in New York and London. She told him about her promotion, and how much she wanted the position, her own house, to feel settled. They talked about music and books, touched on politics, and laughed more than they expected.

They ate, sharing a seafood platter and a bottle of wine, and when a cold wind picked up, they moved inside and sat at the bar, Pasco watching as Aisha ate a generous helping of tiramisu. Around eleven, they left the restaurant and dashed across the road to his car, laughing as the wind blew her dress up to her knees and blew her hair into her eyes.

Aisha leaned her head back on the seat as she watched Pasco walk around the bonnet of the car, stopping to slip a homeless man some cash. Then she saw his hand go to the inside pocket of his jacket and he removed his phone. He caught her eyes through the windscreen and held up his finger, asking her to give him a minute.

After nodding, she leaned her head back and closed her eyes. Despite spending a really lovely evening with Pasco, she had a tension headache behind her eyes. Because Pasco never got sick, she knew he wouldn't have any paracetamol on him and her stash was in her tote bag, which she'd left at Priya's place. A stupid move because she knew, from experience, that any time spent with her family resulted in a migraine-like headache.

What a night! She'd known the party would be tough to navigate, but she'd never anticipated having a what-happened-to-us? conversation with Pasco.

She'd certainly never expected him to apologise, and the memory made her feel warm and a little wonderful.

They'd both been wrong, both made mistakes. As an adult, with time between then and now, she could admit that and maybe move on. Honestly, they'd been too young to marry, too impulsive, drunk on desire, and naive in their belief that love could conquer everything.

She was glad they'd addressed the subject, shooed the elephant out of the room. Oh, they both could've said more, gone a bit deeper, but they'd covered the important bases. And what would change by doing a deep dive into the past? Precisely nothing.

She wasn't the same person she was at nineteen—thank God—and she'd seen changes in Pasco as well. Good changes. And wasn't that the point of life? Growing and changing, acquiring a little more wisdom?

Pasco back then had been balls-to-the-wall, never really slowing down to think, to consider… he'd just set his eyes on a goal and barrelled onward. It seemed to Aisha that Pasco now was more thoughtful, slower to react, to fly off the handle, more considerate. She'd loved him back then, but she *liked* him today, more than she ever had before.

How far he'd come, how far they'd *both* come, was yet to be determined, but what couldn't be denied was their red-hot attraction. They should deny it, ignore it. It would be smarter for them to try and be friends, especially since they needed to cooperate to bring Ro's vision for her St Urban restaurant to fruition. The problem was she didn't see Pasco in a friendly way…no, Pasco made her think of intertwined limbs on cool cotton sheets, masculine hands under her bottom as he slid inside her, filling up those empty, hollow, much neglected feminine places that hadn't seen any action for the longest time. She wanted to feel his lips and teeth on her nipples, his mouth on her stomach. His tongue licking its way down…

Aisha pushed her fingers deeper into her eyes and released a low moan.

Why was her ex the only one who could suck her in like this, who pulled feelings to the surface she didn't want or require? She didn't need the complication of wanting him or wondering whether he wanted her back.

She was out of practice with men, she freely admitted that, but she sensed he did want her. Just a little. Or a lot. And…damn. While she wasn't opposed to the idea of them being friends, it would make life easier, and she liked the notion of them being lovers more. Temporary lovers, she qualified. A couple of nights here and there to scratch the itch, to satisfy her curiosity as to whether her memories lived up to reality.

You're breaking your stay uninvolved rule, Shetty!

This was madness. She had a hotel and a restaurant to establish, a promotion to earn. She didn't have the time or the energy for a love affair.

No, love had left the building a long, long time ago.

But as hard as she tried, she couldn't get the idea of them having a fling out of her head. What would he say if she suggested upgrading their status from friends to friends with temporary benefits? Her stomach fluttered and she knew, just by that small reaction, that this was the worst of ideas. She and Pasco had never been good at simple and she knew that the chance of the situation becoming intensely complicated was high. It was a bad idea, a terrible idea but…

Damn. It was an idea that, like her headache, wouldn't go away.

Pasco ended his call, slid behind the wheel, and closed his door. He turned to look at her and their eyes collided.

She didn't hesitate, just went for what she wanted, and it was blindingly obvious by the heat and lust in his eyes that he wanted her right back. He met her in the moment, his mouth as demanding as hers, and the world faded away, her entire existence narrowed to their lips, his warm hand on her hip, the way his tongue slid into her mouth and wound around hers, sending a buzz of anticipation skittering through her.

She wanted him. So much.

Aisha responded without thinking, spearing her fingers into his hair, running her other hand under his shirt collar to find warm, lovely, masculine skin. She felt his groan, revelled in it, and fumbled for the clasp to free her from her seat belt. It finally popped open and she reached for Pasco again, pulling his mouth back to hers. She hadn't had enough, not nearly enough.

His mouth was hot, spicy with whisky, and

she needed more of his heat, his heady scent, to explore his wide, hard body. How had she gone for so long without him? How had she survived without this pleasure, with not having his hands on her body, making her feel heady, wild, intensely female? Pasco's hand closed over her breast and his thumb swiped her nipple and she pushed off her seat, desperate to get closer. The gear stick pushed into her hip and she cursed the lack of space.

Pasco pulled back suddenly and dropped a curse before running his hand over his face.

'What?' Aisha demanded, half sitting and half kneeling, her breath coming in quick, sharp pants.

Pasco's eyes—hot, wild, and a little feral—met hers. He lifted his hand and created an inch of space between his thumb and index finger. 'I am this far from taking you here and now.'

'I'm that far from letting you,' Aisha admitted. She placed her hand on his hard thigh and released a ragged sigh. 'The way you kiss, I'd forgotten how good you are.'

'Ditto, sweetheart.' Pasco dragged his mouth across hers, but before they could sink into another wild groping session, he placed his hands on her shoulders and pushed her back into her seat.

Aisha looked at the cars passing them, the pedestrians on the boardwalk, feeling dreamy and very buzzy. Her hand remained on Pasco's thigh, and she drew patterns on the fabric of his suit trousers with her thumb. God, she loved touching him.

Pasco gripped her hand and held her fingers still. She slowly turned her head to look at him. 'You don't like that?'

He half grimaced, half smiled. 'I like it far too much and I'm trying my damnedest not to move your hand higher.'

There was no doubt about what he wanted. His face was flushed and his eyes blazed with desire. She dropped her eyes to his lap and if she'd had any doubt, the sight of his erection tenting his trousers would've filled her in.

'You want me,' she murmured, half to herself and half to him.

'Very damn much,' Pasco growled, his fingers squeezing hers. 'I've never been one for making love in cramped cars in public areas, but you make me lose my mind.'

Heat and lust sparked through her at his growly words, coated in frustration. He was such a man and knowing he wanted her thrilled her to her core. She felt powerful and feminine and confident and…

Alive. Her heart was racing and her lungs were heaving. And that was just from a hot-as-lava kiss. If he made love to her, she might just melt into a puddle.

It was a chance she was willing to take. Oh, there were a million reasons why this was a bad idea, and tomorrow she'd probably regret her recklessness but right now? Right now she wanted more, she wanted everything he could give her.

Aisha turned in her seat to look at his handsome profile, and her heart skipped a beat. 'You have a house around here, right?'

His head whipped around to look at her, hope sparking in his eyes. 'My apartment in Fresnaye is about ten minutes from here if I drive fast.'

'Floor it, Pas.'

He gently gripped her jaw with his big hand and her eyes slammed into his. 'If I take you home, you will be naked ten seconds after I get you in my front door, sweetheart.'

She gripped his strong wrist and sent him what she hoped was a seductive smile. 'Well, I hope so. I wasn't asking you to take me home to play Scrabble.'

Pasco dropped a hard, open-mouthed kiss on her lips before pulling back and hitting the button to fire up his powerful engine. Backing out of the parking space, he skilfully and quickly navigated the still busy streets to the luxurious suburb of Fresnaye.

He made it to his place in seven minutes.

of the parking space, he ERED, and once they round the all bury streets to the outskirts subured of Freespa.

The eight mile drive took seventeen minutes

CHAPTER SEVEN

PASCO PARKED HIS car in one of the four bays in his garage and led her from the garage to his front door. Aisha quickened her pace to keep up with him, laughing when he fumbled the in-putting of the code to open his eight-foot-high front door. He cursed, slowed down, and jabbed at the buttons again and the door clicked open. Pasco pushed her ahead of him, kicked the door shut with his foot, and then the hall lights came on, illuminating his tense face.

Instead of reaching for her, he pushed his hand into his trouser pockets and stared at her, his eyes darting from her mouth to her eyes and back again. A muscle ticced in his jaw and she could see the tension in his wide shoulders, in the way he held his big body.

Why was he just standing there, looking at her? Why wasn't he doing anything? If he didn't kiss her soon, she might lose her nerve…

She rubbed her hand down her hip, suddenly nervous. 'Why are you just standing there?'

'Back then, it was normally me, *always* me, who initiated lovemaking. You, going for what you want, is a hell of a turn-on. I want you so damn much.'

Great, lovely, she was happy to hear it, but could they get on with it? Aisha stepped forward but stopped when he held up his hand. She raised her eyebrows at him, impatient.

Hesitation flickered in his eyes. 'Are you completely sure?' he asked. 'Because, if we start, I'm not backing off.'

Now that was nonsense, she knew that, no matter how far they went, she could call a halt to what they were doing, and he'd stop.

Though the chances of her doing that were honestly less than zero. She wanted him now, tonight. She didn't know if it was a good idea or whether she'd regret this in the morning, but she didn't care. For once she was going to seize the moment, go with the flow, carpe-the-hell-diem.

'Aish—'

Hesitation still lurked in his eyes—did he think they were crossing too big a line here?— but honestly, she was past caring. 'Shut up, Pas.'

Pasco's eyes didn't leave hers as she stepped towards him to slide her hand under his jacket, above his heart. It was thudding hard, another sign of how much he wanted her, wanted this. She ran her hand down his shirt, marvelling at the muscles under his shirt, the heat radiating off him.

He stayed statue still as she pushed his jacket off his shoulders, allowing it to drop to the slate floor beneath her feet. She had a brief thought that she wanted to see his house, explore his home, but that could come later. She had more important things to do with her time right now.

Aisha looked up at him and stood on her tiptoes to skim her mouth across his before dropping back down to pull his shirt from the waistband of his trousers. Torturing them both, she slowly undid the buttons of his shirt and pushed it apart, placing her mouth on his skin, tasting him. Her hands moved up his chest, over his shoulders as she kissed his flat nipple and dragged her nose through his light chest hair. His arms were big, bulging with muscles as she pulled one hand from his pocket, then the other.

He kept them by his sides as her fingers moved to his belt buckle. She glanced up and the intensity in his moss-green eyes sent a bolt of electricity through her, igniting every nerve ending she possessed.

'Touch me, Pas, I need you to,' Aisha said, lifting her hand to touch his jaw.

Her command—or was it a plea?—released

him from his self-imposed stance and his arm
encircled her waist and yanked her into him. He
bent his knees and took her mouth in a hard kiss
that was just this side of savage.

Aisha loved it, loved the need she tasted on his
tongue. He wanted her as much as she did him
and the thought made her head spin.

With her mouth under his, she pushed his shirt
off his shoulders, laughing when it hooked on his
wrists. Pasco cursed, and ripped his cuffs apart,
and buttons pinged across the hall floor. When
he was free, he took her mouth again and hiked
her long dress up, releasing a groan of apprecia-
tion when his hand encircled the top of her thigh.

He pulled away and buried his face in her
neck. 'You taste, feel, so good.'

Aisha arched her neck as his mouth moved
down her throat and her chest, and she held her
breath as he nuzzled her nipple through her dress
and bra. Frustrated with the barriers between
them, she quickly undid her belt and, grabbing
the edges of her dress, pulled it up and over her
head and dropped it. She stood in his hallway in
her skimpy black panties and lacy transparent
bra and watched Pasco's eyes darken. He slowly,
far too slowly, pulled the edge of one lacy bra
cup aside and stared at her nipple, before bending his knees to take her into his mouth. She
whimpered and combed her fingers through his

hair, arching her back to encourage him to take more, do more.

Pasco straightened and pressed his thumb into her bottom lip. 'Bedroom, now.'

She couldn't wait that long. 'Here, now.'

'You're sure?' Pasco asked her. 'If we stay here, it's going to be hard. And fast. And it'll be up against the wall.'

She nodded; that was what she wanted this first time again with him. Hot and fast and wild. Out of control. 'Works for me.'

Pasco nodded and reached into his back pocket and withdrew his wallet. He yanked out cards and cash, plastic and notes falling to the floor as he searched for a condom. He pulled one out, dropped the leather wallet, and reached for her, sliding his hands down the back of her panties.

His kiss was all-consuming, limitless, and Aisha pushed her hands between them to undo his belt, then his zip. She pushed her hands inside and there he was, hot and oh-so-hard. So very Pasco.

From there on, time stood still as hands streaked over flesh, mouths followed. They didn't take the time to undress fully, her panties were pushed aside, his trousers fell halfway down his hips, just enough for him to move. Aisha slid the condom over his long length and a second after she was done, Pasco grabbed the backs of her legs, ordered her to wrap her legs around his, and slid into her in one fluid, fantastic, soul-touching stroke.

He groaned and leaned her back against the nearest wall, his forehead on hers, his face a mask of concentration.

He rocked, she responded, igniting a million detonators, setting off a chain reaction of need and want and passion. Chemistry was too tame a word for what he did to her, how he made her feel. Aisha gasped as he rocked deeper into her, she tightened her legs and pushed down and, deep down inside her, stars collided and galaxies exploded.

God, she'd missed him so much. Missed this. Missed him in her body.

And in her life.

Early the next morning Aisha left Pasco sleeping in his king-sized bed and, after pulling on his button-down shirt, padded across his enormous bedroom, skirted the small lounge within his enormous sleeping quarters, and glanced right and…

Stopped.

How could she not?

The sky was awash with shades of pink and purple, accompanied by the music of the sea drumming the rocks below his deck. Entranced by the magical colours, Aisha walked over to frameless folding doors, found the mechanism to slide them open, grateful when the doors opened without a whisper of a sound.

She needed a moment alone, to stand in the magical light and bliss out on the incredible view.

Aisha walked onto the patio running the length of the apartment, skirted the long lap pool, stopping to dip her toe into the water—it was heated, of course—and leaned her elbows on the glass balustrade, also unframed. She recognised the beach to her right as being Moses Beach, a highly desirable location. From Pasco's apartment one could enjoy outstanding views of the sea, white sand, and the incredible tip of Africa sky.

The only thing that would make this view any better would be a cup of coffee.

And, possibly, a lobotomy.

Exquisite sunrise or not, there was no getting around the fact she'd slept with her ex last night, the man she needed to work with for the next month. Slept with? Ha, no! She'd devoured him, all but climbed inside him. They'd started in the hallway, moved onto the open-plan reception lounge—she recalled massive cream couches and outstanding, vibrant, oversized art—and finally made it to his bedroom, where they'd rolled around on his California king. Lord, they'd even shared his shower, exchanging long languid kisses and indulging in some heavy petting.

Aisha gently banged her forehead on the edge of the glass balustrade, wondering if she'd completely lost her mind. What had she been thinking? Had she been thinking at all?

She'd been here before, been enthralled by Pasco, and she hadn't liked playing second fiddle to his career and his priorities. She'd vowed never to give him—any man—that sort of power over her again. She didn't trust love, couldn't rely on it—it was a lesson her family had taught her and Pasco had reinforced—so she had to focus on what she could control, what she could rely on. And that was her work. Becoming involved with Pasco, even at a purely superficial level, would be a distraction from what she needed to do at St Urban.

She didn't have the time for a fling, for a lover, and she couldn't afford to be distracted. She was so close to the goal she'd set for herself when she first joined Lintel & Lily all those years ago.

She would not let her intense and inconvenient attraction to her ex-husband and current work colleague impact her professionalism. She was better than that. She'd obey the rules.

Aisha looked at the oversized men's watch on her wrist, saw that it was just past six, and thought about calling for an Uber to run her back to Priya's place so she could collect her car and then she'd head back to Franschhoek. She wanted to avoid any early-morning awkwardness with Pasco and she thought putting a little time and distance between them would be a very good thing.

Running again, Shetty?

She pulled a face at the still gorgeous sky— lighter now—and sighed. She was an adult and should be able to have a reasonable, intelligent conversation with the man who'd rocked her world last night. She was sure, well, mostly sure, she wouldn't do anything stupid, like make love to him on one of those two-seater lounges as the sun rose. One night and she was already looking for another Pasco-induced high. Another and she might become addicted. Aisha sighed.

No, she wouldn't run, but when she mustered the courage to walk back into his bedroom and wake him up—but only after a cup of coffee or three—she'd tell him that their sleeping together was a lapse in judgement, a step out of time, that it couldn't happen again.

They had to work together and to do that they needed to be professional and uninvolved.

She would not let her attraction to her husband—*ex*-husband dammit!—impact her work. She had a promotion to secure, a life to lock in, a house to buy.

She'd learned one lesson from Pasco—along with never making quick decisions and that love was a farce—and that was to put her career first.

He was, after all, brilliant at doing just that.

'Pretty sunrise.'

His voice behind her made her skin prickle, and Aisha turned around to look at him, standing in the doorway to the open-plan lounge, two coffee cups in his hands, steam rising from the surface. He wore a pair of lightweight cotton trousers and his pale grey T-shirt clung to his broad chest. His golden-brown hair looked messy, his three-day-old beard was thicker this morning and he had a pillow crease across his right cheek.

He looked amazing.

Pasco skirted the outdoor furniture, walked over to her, and pushed a cup into her hands. He lifted his to the sky in a silent toast.

'It was lovelier earlier, streaks of deep pinks and purples and golds,' Aisha told him, wrapping her hands around the mug.

Pasco sipped before responding. 'I think this is the best place to watch the sunrise, better even than Table Mountain. I remember visiting a school friend's house in this area when I was about ten or eleven and seeing a sunrise like this. I vowed that I would some day own a house right on the beach.'

Aisha looked over the balustrade on the rocks below. Yep, once Pasco set his sights on a goal, he never relented. Yes, she'd walked out on him, but she couldn't help thinking that he'd let her go so easily that he hadn't fought for their relationship—hadn't tried to talk to her about coming back, hadn't followed her home. Their relationship wasn't something he'd put a lot of effort into. The thought still made her heart hurt.

That was why they would never be anything more than lovers. She'd never hand her heart over to him again.

'I saw the sunset earlier, I woke up as you left the bed,' Paso told her. 'I've been watching you for the past fifteen minutes.'

She didn't know what to say to that, how to respond.

'So, when are you going to talk to me about rules, tell me that this isn't a good idea, that we are work colleagues who shouldn't complicate their lives by getting physically involved, that this was a one-night thing?'

God! She hated it when he read her mind. She fought the urge to either smack or kiss that know-it-all look off his face. But since he'd opened that door, she'd walk on in. 'I don't have to because you said it for me,' she pointed out, pleased at her super-reasonable tone.

'We're adults, Aisha, we can separate sex

from work,' Pasco told her, his tone abrupt. 'One doesn't have anything to do with the other.'

'Didn't you say that you were avoiding me because of our attraction? Because you kept thinking about taking me to bed?'

'Fair point,' he conceded.

Aisha looked at him across the rim of her coffee cup. 'We have a history, Pasco, one that doesn't get wiped away with one hot-as-fire encounter. We're divorced, and one night of conversation doesn't put our past to bed. I also need to work with you, and adding sex makes it complicated.'

Pasco sighed and rested his mug on the balustrade. He frowned and rubbed his hand over his face. 'Do you want to have another conversation about the past?'

'I can see that you don't,' Aisha retorted.

'What more is there to say? I was bossy and domineering, didn't spend enough time with you, and didn't make an effort to give you what you needed. You didn't explain what you needed and then you bailed, leaving just a note.'

She wanted to tell him that, if he loved her, he should've *known* she was unhappy. That he didn't look hard enough, that he didn't *see* her.

Before she could lash out, and she wanted to, he spoke again. 'Aish, guys are not good at subtext, we don't read between the lines. I'm a straightforward guy. I might've understood how miserable you were if you sat me down, looked me in the eyes, and used small words. Words like "I'm leaving unless you get your crap together", "I'm miserable", "help me figure this out".' He shrugged. 'But maybe, because I was too young or too conceited or too lazy, it was easier to tell myself that whatever you were feeling would blow over.'

A part of her wanted to blame everything on him; her ego wanted Pasco to be at fault. But that wasn't fair.

Aisha watched as a wave covered the rocks with white foam and gathered her courage to explain. It would be hard, but that wasn't an excuse to duck the issue.

'Everyone in my family is profoundly intelligent and so very erudite, Pasco. They are also intensely rational and, being scientists, none of them is driven by emotion. I am the cuckoo in the nest. I found it difficult to express myself verbally. And I felt everything… I was a walking, talking miasma of emotion.'

She forced herself to continue. 'I'd tried to talk to them but, because we came at issues from entirely different directions—rational thinking versus emotional—we rarely agreed. I invariably walked away from every conversation feeling less than, unseen and, sometimes, stupid.

'I wasn't good at expressing myself so I stopped,' she added. 'I learned to shut down, to keep my thoughts and feelings to myself. Not only with them, but with everyone. I guess I carried that over into our marriage, stupidly thinking that, because you loved me, you'd know how I felt and what I was thinking.'

His hand drifted down her arm. 'You don't seem to have a problem communicating in a business setting,' Pasco commented.

'In the early days with Lintel & Lily, I was passed over for promotion, despite being damn good at my job, not once, but twice. Miles, my boss, pulled me aside and told me that if I wanted to move up, I'd have to learn to state what I wanted, to start communicating better.' She shrugged, remembering how hard, and how frightening, it had been to break those habits from her childhood. She'd come a long way.

Aisha knew his eyes were on her face, could feel his heat, smell his divine scent. She felt exposed and a little raw. She needed to put some distance between them, to wrap her head around everything that had happened: them sleeping together, the part she'd played in their divorce, how they were going to work together with the desire bubbling between them.

She needed space now, and started to walk away, but Pasco snagging her shirt impeded her progress. She whipped around and scowled at him. 'What?'

'Where are you going?'

'Inside to get dressed and then to call an Uber. I want to go back to St Urban. I have work to do.'

'You're pissed off with me,' Pasco growled, frustration in his eyes.

She wanted to agree, but her innate honesty had her shaking her head. 'Actually, I'm more annoyed with myself than with you.' She shrugged. 'I want you to be solely responsible for our marriage imploding and knowing I played a bigger part than I thought is hard to accept.'

Pasco's smile was tender as he pushed his fingers in her hair above her ear, raking back her hair. 'We can dissect the past, take it apart bit by bit, but it won't make a damn bit of difference. What if we decide to forgive each other, forgive our younger, dumber selves and move on?'

She held his strong wrist. 'Pasco…'

He dropped his head to nuzzle her temple. 'I don't want to fight with you, Aisha. We were kids, we made mistakes, both of us. But here we are, older and, hopefully, a little wiser. Let's move on, sweetheart.'

He rested his forehead on hers. 'I'm sorry I hurt you, Aisha.'

What else could she say but… 'I'm sorry I hurt you too.' And she was. Aisha sighed and the cracks in her heart started to knit themselves back together. There'd be scars, but those chasms would heal.

His too, she hoped.

'Spend the day with me,' Pasco suggested, his lips brushing hers. 'I want to drink my coffee and watch the sunrise with you in my arms. Then I want to make you breakfast and take you back to bed. Give me today, sweetheart, one day where we have no past, no future, no worries, no agendas.'

God, she was tempted. So tempted. She wanted that more than she wanted to breathe or for her heart to keep beating. But playing hooky, from life and reality, was a risk and one that might come back to bite her. It might make her want more, far more than she could ever have.

But it had been so long, years and years, since she'd allowed herself the pleasure of a step out of time, to take a day for herself, to spoil herself. And spending the day with a man who made her heart race, her skin prickle, and her mouth water was the ultimate in spoiling herself.

She didn't shop, she didn't take spa days, she didn't take vacations. She worked. She could do this, she was allowed to do this, and, being a big girl, she'd accept the consequences.

'One day, Aisha. Come play with me.'

When he looked at her like that, those deep

green eyes temptation personified, she couldn't resist. And why on earth would any woman want to?

After breakfast—fluffy blueberry pancakes with honeycomb and bacon butter—and another round of soul-stealing, languid, lovely lovemaking, Pasco bundled her into his shower and told her he'd be back in half an hour. She showered, pulled on the long-sleeved T-shirt he'd left her and climbed back into his bed, buried her nose in his pillow, and drifted off to sleep. She woke up an hour later and saw a pile of clothing at the bottom of the bed.

Yawning, she pawed through the pile, finding designer jeans and a white, men's style button-down shirt, a soft leather jacket, belt, shoes, socks, and even underwear. And the sizes were spot on. She dressed and, carrying the low-heeled boots and socks, walked down the hallway, back into the entrance hall—that wall would always have a soft spot in her heart—and into the lounge area. The sun was shining, and Pasco had opened all the doors leading onto the entertainment area and she could hear the waves crashing onto the rocks below. This was a brilliant example of bringing the outside in. Wide awake and not in a sex-induced haze, she could take in the details of his exquisitely decorated apartment, the squishy cream couches with colourful cushions, the enormous flat-screen TV, the wall of books. Sculptures and paintings, some old, some new, added character.

Dropping her boots to the Persian carpet, she padded past a ten-seater indoor dining table—there was another one outside—and found a gourmet kitchen with its cheffy ovens, upmarket appliances, and a huge fridge.

Pasco stood at the island, expertly chopping vegetables. He smiled at her, and Aisha felt her heart roll over. 'Don't you have minions to chop vegetables for you these days?' she asked.

'I do, but I like to keep my hand in,' Pasco told her, his knife flying even as he kept his eyes on her.

Sliding onto a bar stool, she sniffed the garlic-and-herb-scented air. 'What are you making? It smells delicious.'

'I thought I'd test out an idea I had for a recipe while you slept,' he replied, leaning across the island to drop a quick kiss on her lips. He dropped his eyes to her chest and waved the knife at her shirt. 'I'm glad the clothes fit.'

'Thanks for getting them for me,' Aisha said. 'I'll pay you back.'

He ignored her suggestion and Aisha looked around the apartment. 'This is one hell of a place, Kildare. How many bedrooms?'

'Three plus a study, wine cellar, gym, and sauna upstairs.'

Wow. 'When did you buy it?'

He dumped the diced onions into the pot sitting on a sleek stovetop embedded in the island. 'Ah, when I sold my New York place. I came home, looked for a place on the beach, saw this, and put in an offer on the same day.'

'Thereby obtaining yet another of your goals,' Aisha stated. She saw the bottle of orange juice and poured some into the glass he'd been using. She took a long sip and realised that it was freshly juiced. Marvellous.

Pasco nodded, his thoughts far away. 'I guess the house I saw so long ago made such an impression on me because my friend's family had so much and we had so little.' The corners of his mouth lifted in a self-deprecating smile. 'I was always competitive and I didn't like coming second-best.'

Aisha lowered her glass, trying to make sense of his words. 'I don't understand. You come from money, your dad is one of the wealthiest men in the valley, your mum is a doctor.'

Pasco stirred the onions before gripping the edges of the counter, straightening his arms. 'The man I call my dad, the man I consider to be my dad, is my stepdad. I took John's surname the year I turned thirteen, the year I went to high school. And yeah, he's wealthy, but before we met him we were, at times, dirt poor.'

'I don't understand,' Aisha said, her thoughts swirling. 'Your mum is a doctor.'

'It's an ugly story, Aisha,' he said as he cleaned his board of onion skins.

But it was a story, one he hadn't told before, one she didn't know. Despite their wedding vows, she didn't know much, or anything, about his early childhood, and the fact he was telling her this now both intrigued and scared her. What did it mean? Was this his way of deepening their friendship?

She didn't understand...

Pasco stood up, switched off the stove, and wiped his hands on a snowy white kitchen cloth. 'My father, also known as the sperm donor, studied business management at university, but dropped out in his second year. Shortly after Mum graduated they married, and a year after that I was born. My mum was the breadwinner in our family, so she worked and my dad stayed at home and took care of us and our finances.'

Anger and devastation sparked in his eyes, and Aisha resisted the urge to walk around the island to comfort him, but knew that if she did anything but sit still and listen, he'd clam up.

After a long silence, Pasco spoke again. 'My mum earned good money and my dad spent it on cracked business schemes. God, he tried everything, from making shoelaces to selling mobile phones. He had a food truck and then a butchery. He sold coins off the internet and antique furniture.'

'I'm sensing he wasn't good with money,' Aisha quietly stated, keeping any censure out of her voice.

'He had the attention span of a fly and couldn't stick to anything for more than a minute. He'd borrow money, using my mum's credit, start up a business, and when he was bored, packed it in. Two months later, he'd borrow more money and the cycle would repeat itself.'

Aisha cocked her head to the side. 'Why didn't your mum put a stop to it?'

Pasco rubbed the back of his neck. 'My lovely, stunningly intelligent mother was a fool when it came to my father. She loved him, wildly and intensely. He brainwashed or nagged or conned her into believing that love had to equal complete trust. In what she now admits was the stupidest mistake of her life, she gave him power of attorney over her financial affairs. For someone like my dad, that was like giving a teenager a limitless credit card and dropping her off at the mall. He managed to keep our money troubles from her for the longest time, but I heard his conversations, I knew something was wrong. But he told me not to bother our mum with it, that she was stressed, tired and he was taking care of everything.'

'But he didn't.'

Pasco's mouth thinned. 'No, he didn't.'

His eyes turned distant and dull. Something major happened, an event that kicked them sideways and upended his world. 'What did he do, Pas?'

Pasco raked his fingers through his hair and when he looked at her, she saw the regret in his eyes. It was obvious to Aisha he was wishing he hadn't opened this can of worms, that he could back away and return to normality. Whatever that was.

But this was the first time ever—and how sad was that?—that she'd burrowed beneath his everything-is-peachy surface and she wanted to know how that chapter of his life ended.

Aisha stared at him, willing him to open up, to confide in her. She didn't say anything, knowing he either would or wouldn't confide in her, nothing she did or said would make him do something he didn't want to do.

'His creditors finally caught up with him,' Pasco stated, sounding a little robotic. 'My birthday is a week before Christmas, and they threw me a birthday party. I invited everybody I knew, girls, guys, old friends, new friends. We lived in a nice house…not fancy, but it had this big pool…so we decided to have a pool party. They hired a DJ, and it was the best party ever…up until the debt collectors stormed in and started loading up our furniture and putting tow hitches on the cars.'

Aisha put her hand to her mouth. Dear God.

'They took everything that wasn't nailed down, anything that had even the smallest value. My boombox and our PlayStation, paintings, the jewellery my mum inherited from her mum and grandmother.'

'Why did they take her property?' Aisha demanded.

'My parents were married in community of property so everything was fair game,' Pasco explained. 'We were left with our pets, two cats and three dogs, and a suitcase of clothes each.'

'And this all happened at the party?' Aisha asked, horrified.

'Yeah, I remember an argument between the DJ and the collection agents because they tried to take his mixing equipment. Some of the girls were crying, the boys were laughing. One of our dogs bit one of the removers.'

He tried to smile, but there was no amusement behind the action. 'Eventually, everyone cleared out and we were left in this house with, I kid you not, nothing. Not even a kettle. There was food and they put it onto the kitchen floor. But we couldn't do anything with it because there wasn't a stove, or pots or pans.'

Aisha held her hands to her cheeks, horrified. 'How did your mum respond?'

Anger, hot and bright, flashed in his eyes. 'I'll never forget my mum sitting on the floor of her empty lounge and staring up at my dad. She asked him how much money was in the bank and he said that they were overdrawn. She listed every account, and he answered the same way every time, that there was nothing. The credit cards were maxed out. He had a little cash in his wallet, she had none.'

Pasco folded his arms across his chest and stared past her to the amazing view outside. 'Can we stop talking about this now?'

'Tell me the rest, Pas. Please.'

He looked at her, desperation and humiliation in his eyes. 'I can't, I'm done,' he replied, his voice hoarse. 'I haven't thought about it for years, talked about it since it happened.' He rolled his shoulders back and reached for the pot on the stove, tossing the contents into the waste disposal. 'I'm feeling claustrophobic, let's get out of here.'

She looked at the wide expanse of the deck, the sunlight streaming into his apartment, and felt as if she were standing on the edge of the world, light and free. His house was linked to the land, the sea, and the sky and there was nothing claustrophobic about it.

Pasco wasn't running away from his place but his past, the memories. And she could understand that. He was so successful now, so financially secure that being reminded of that awful time in his life—how out of control he felt, so helpless—had made him feel jumpy.

A part of her wanted to push, to dig deeper, but he'd given her what he could, and that was far more than he ever had before.

She nodded and when he held out his hand, she placed hers in his. 'Where are we going?'

'Out.' He gestured to the bright sunshine and the intense, deep, glorious blue sky. 'It's a stunning day, we are together, playing hooky, so does it matter?'

When he put it like that, she didn't think it did.

CHAPTER EIGHT

Aisha broke off a piece of fish and looked at him from her side of the picnic table overlooking the wide, stunning beach. Their helmets rested on the wooden bench next to them and icy bottles of beer dripped condensation onto the wooden table.

She'd pulled her hair back into a loose knot at the back of her neck and the sunglasses he'd lent her kept slipping down her nose. She had a grease smudge on the side of her mouth, and she kept making take-me-now noises as she worked her way through the greasy but fantastic fish and chips.

After spilling his soul earlier—those brown-black eyes were like a truth drug—Pasco vowed to keep the rest of their day fun and light-hearted. Instead of taking one of his three cars, he'd handed her a helmet and put her behind him on his powerful Ducati, thinking it was a truly excellent day to drive the magnificent Chapman's

Peak road. Aisha just smiled, plastered her chest against his back, wrapped her slim arms around him, and, following his lead, leaned into the corners, confident in his ability to keep her safe on the dangerous road.

When they stopped, at a viewpoint or for coffee, and she removed her helmet and his sunglasses, he saw excitement sparkling in her eyes and he wondered how he'd lived his life for so long—in both New York and, before that, in London—without days like these. Easy days, loving days, days he never wanted to end. Hearing her laughter coming over his intercom system and enjoying her relaxed body behind him, he'd carried on driving up the coast, eventually stopping for lunch in Pringle Bay, a charming coastal village situated on the famous Whale Route. Instead of a fancy restaurant, he'd headed for a small fish and chips shop and ordered them a takeaway lunch. He wasn't disappointed with the meal; the hake was perfectly cooked, he thought, licking salt off his fingers, tipping his face up to enjoy the autumn sun.

'God, this is good,' she muttered, picking up another chip and waving it around. 'Tell me about Pringle Bay. I've never been here before.'

Pasco gestured to a mountain to his right. 'The town is surrounded by mountains on three sides and the ocean and the bay, as you can see, is awesome.'

Aisha wiped her hands on a paper serviette and took a sip of her beer. 'Who was Mr Pringle?'

Pasco smiled at her. 'That would be Rear Admiral Thomas Pringle to you, sweetheart. The town was established in the late 1700s. There's also a cave around here, which was used by prisoners and runaway slaves as a hideaway in the eighteenth century.'

Aisha's eyes widened. 'Seriously? Can we see it?'

He shook his head. 'It's on private ground and is hard to find. It's in an inlet washed by the sea and you get to it by a rope between rock walls. I think I remember something about someone in the 1890s finding skeletons in the cave.'

Aisha turned sideways on the bench, lifted her feet, and wrapped her arms around her legs. He was happy to sit in the sun, drink his beer and watch her.

Pasco tipped his bottle to his mouth, mentally running through the last twenty-four hours. Sex with Aisha had been wonderful a decade ago, but last night it had been nothing short of spectacular. She was less inhibited—thank God—than she'd been at nineteen, he more patient, and the combination was explosive. He could still taste her on his lips, could smell her scent, feel her soft skin under her hands…feel himself stirring once again.

He wanted her again. He didn't think there'd be a time when he'd ever not want Aisha. He was drawn to her in a primal, moth-to-a-flame way—wanting her was in his DNA.

He could understand the physical connection—she was a stunning woman who made men's heads turn, their attraction was understandable—but he didn't understand why he'd told her about his dad, about his life before his family moved to Franschhoek. He never spoke to anyone about what his dad put them through, preferred to forget it, to not think about it at all. As far as he was concerned, his life started when they moved to Franschhoek, and John started dating his mum.

But he'd told Aisha about his life before this life, and he wondered why he'd done that. He'd had many lovers since their divorce, but he always kept things simple, not delving into their lives and keeping them from digging into his. When they pushed for more, for a deeper connection, he always, always ended things, stating that he didn't have the time, that his life was too chaotic for a love affair. A few called him on his emotional unavailability, but he didn't allow their tears or anger to affect him.

He didn't talk. Okay, sure, he'd got through

two conversations about their marriage with Aisha—yay him!—but those were super-necessary, had to be done so that they could move on. But what was the point of harping on the past? It couldn't be changed by some back-and-forth exchange of words.

Then, strangely, he'd opened up about his dad. But he still hadn't been able to tell Aisha the worst of it. Only his mum, his brother, and his stepdad John knew the next chapter of that go-dawful saga.

'It's very pretty here. As lovely as St Urban.'

'Mmm. I looked at buying property here when I returned from the States,' Pasco told her.

'To do what?' Aisha asked, turning her head to look at him.

He shrugged. 'I had this idea of buying a plot of land, establishing greenhouses, and running a small farm-to-table place, little work, no pressure. Living the simple life, you know.'

Her eyebrows rose, as if she couldn't conceive the notion.

'I know, right? I don't blame you for your disbelief. I would've gone off my head in six months.'

'Actually, I'm surprised by the wistfulness I heard in your voice. It sounds like that's something you'd like to do.'

There she went again, seeing through his layers. 'It's not me, Aisha. I do better in high-pressure environments.'

'But do you like it?'

He frowned at her. 'Sorry?'

'Do you like running your swish restaurant at The Vane, Binta, the restaurant in Franschhoek? Does it make you happy?'

The returns, the money in the bank did. The security it gave him made him very happy indeed. Being successful, not following in his father's reckless, unsuccessful footsteps, was all that mattered.

'Yeah.'

'Wow, don't go overboard with your response, Kildare.'

Pasco wiped his hands, bundled up their packets, and tossed them into a nearby rubbish bin. Instead of retaking his seat, he walked around the table and sat behind Aisha, his legs on either side of the bench and her hips. He wound his arm across her torso and pulled her back so her back rested on his chest.

She gripped his arm in her hand and sighed. 'It's such a perfect day. I could sit here for the rest of the day, drinking beers and watching the waves, hoping to see a whale.'

'Better chance of that in June,' he told her, burying his nose in her sweet-smelling hair. He looked over her shoulder at his watch and saw that it was past three. He had a conference call scheduled at five with the same investor who helped him set up Pasco's, Manhattan seven years ago. Hank wasn't the type for out-of-the-blue chats and Pasco suspected he'd found an interesting space or stumbled on a new concept for a restaurant.

The restaurant would be in New York because Hank was Brooklyn born and bred and Manhattan was his playground. Hank still hadn't forgiven Pasco for bailing on the Big Apple—in his eyes, it was the only place to be—and he'd made it his life mission to pull Pasco back to the city. Maybe it was time to consider doing that; his local restaurants were now exceptionally well run and he didn't need to be here any more.

He'd see what Hank had to say…

The only thing that made him hesitate was this woman in his arms.

He tensed up, immediately dismissing that thought. *Do not overthink this, and don't get sucked into the romance of this, Kildare, it was one night, one great day. A step out of time.* He wasn't young and idealistic any more and knew that one night in her arms didn't mean anything. It was great sex—they'd always been compatible physically—and some laughs. It was a way to get each other out of their system. They'd had their chance and there was no going back.

She'd get St Urban and the pop-up restaurant up and running and then she'd go back to…where?

'When you are done with St Urban and get your promotion, where do you intend living?'

He felt her small shrug. 'After my not-so-fun reunion with my family last night, I think it's best if I stay as far away from them as possible, so probably London.'

If he went to New York, it was only a six-hour flight between the cities. It took half a day to fly from London to Cape Town. God, was he really thinking that far ahead? He hadn't even spoken to Hank yet…

But if he wanted to keep on seeing her after her time ended at St Urban, provided they hadn't crashed and burned by then, London and New York were more doable. At least the cities were in the same hemisphere.

One date, one night together and he was already making plans, just as he had ten years ago. He'd seen her in that pub, decided she was going to be his, and set out to make it happen. With other women, he made a move, mostly got what he wanted—a hook-up or a fling—and moved on, not letting her affect his life in any material way.

He was like his dad that way and the thought pissed him off. Going for what he wanted without considering how his actions affected others. The thought made him feel a little sick.

He wouldn't be like that with Aisha; he refused to repeat his past mistakes. He'd be better than his dad, better than he'd been before. She made him feel more, want to be more...

Yeah, she heated his blood, but she also calmed his mind and inspired him to be a better man. But God, walking around with a heart high on emotion *terrified* him.

So he'd tread slowly, slow the hell down, take a breath, try to be goddamn sensible around her.

Talking about sensible...

'We should think about getting back, Aish.'

She sighed, kissed his wrist, and dropped her knees. 'I know. I still need to get my car from Priya and get back to St Urban.'

'And I have a conference call and I need to inspect management accounts.'

Aisha stood up, Pasco followed her to her feet, and they walked towards his matt black Ducati. He handed her her helmet and pulled his sunglasses off the top of her head. 'We need to talk about the restaurant.'

Aisha cocked her head to look at him.

'I realised that if I give you some solid time, we could just get it done. I'll rearrange my schedule so I can give it a few full days next week.'

Aisha nodded. 'That would be great. If we

could work over the weekends, then I could work on St Urban during the week.'

He shook his head. 'Weekends are normally busy for me, and we're catering the Tempest-Vane ball in a few weekends. Are you going?' Aisha shook her head. 'Uh…no. What ball?'

'It's their annual ball to raise funds for their foundation.'

'You're confusing me with your A-list friends, and I'm far too busy to socialise.'

Pasco sent her a lazy smile. 'Honey, nobody is ever too busy for a Tempest-Vane ball. I'll arrange an invitation for you—you should come.'

He saw the hesitation on her face. 'You should meet the Tempest-Vanes. They would be great contacts for you.'

'Is this a business invitation or are you asking me to be your date, Kildare?' Aisha asked before slinging one leg over his bike and scooting back.

Yeah, he didn't blame her for sounding a little pissed off. 'I'd love you to be my date, but I have to run the kitchen, so I'll only be able to join you around ten-thirty, eleven. I'll arrange for you to sit with Muzi and Ro, and the Tempest-Vanes.'

He saw her indecision and sighed. 'Hey, I'm cooking and the menu is stunning. You know you can't resist my food.'

She didn't smile. 'Do you want me there?'

God help him, he did. 'Yes.'

'Okay, then, it's a date.' She lifted her finger and sent him a cheeky smile. 'But I'm only coming for the food.'

He grinned. No, she wasn't. 'Noted. And when can we get together to discuss Ro's pop-up restaurant?'

'I have a quietish day tomorrow, but I suppose that won't suit you?'

His heart leapt at the idea of seeing her again so soon. And because Mondays were normally a slow day, he nodded. He had some meetings, but they could be rearranged. 'That'll work. I'll be with you by nine.' He dropped a kiss on her lips before helping to secure her helmet.

He settled himself on his bike, felt her arms around his waist, and sighed. He didn't want this day to end; he liked being with her, having her in touching distance, hearing her voice, smelling her scent. He loved the sex, but the simplicity of her company was as wonderful.

She was still lovely, a little sweet, a lot sassier. Stronger too. There was definitely a balance between them that hadn't been there before. He could, if he needed to, lean on her, knew she wouldn't, this time around, break. Or run. He was less arrogant, he hoped, she a bit more assertive, and he liked them better now, as individuals and as a couple.

This could, if they chose to let it, grow into

something…special. Intense. Meaningful and important.

And that terrified him.

Pasco, unfortunately, only made it to St Urban on Tuesday morning. Yeah, he was a day late, but on Sunday evening, after his call with Hank—and yes, he did want Pasco to fly over to inspect a building for a new restaurant—he checked in with his chef de cuisine at The Vane Hotel and, two minutes into his video call, realised Davit was either sick or getting sick. His sickly pallor, tired, dull eyes and his croaky voice made Pasco think his right-hand man was on the point of collapse.

Pasco, worried that Davit would infect the rest of his staff with whatever bug he was carrying, told him to go home. But Davit refused, telling him that two of his station chefs were off work, thanks to the same bug. Pasco didn't hesitate and headed straight for the restaurant. He told Davit to beat it, pulled on his chef's jacket, and got to work. Davit wasn't ready to come back to work on Monday, but luckily, professed himself well enough to resume work on Tuesday.

'Hi,' he said when Aisha waved him into her office. He caught a glance at her face and internally winced. Tight lips, narrowed eyes, clenched jaw...he didn't need to be a rocket scientist to realise she was ticked.

Pasco sat down in the chair opposite her and placed his ankle on his other knee as he inspected the loose braid running along the side of her head. With tendrils falling out, it was a soft and feminine look and was in direct contrast to her flat eyes and irritated expression.

'Are you okay?'

Aisha didn't look at him and neither did she reply. Unease rippled up his spine. He thought he'd try again.

'Ready to head down to the cellar?' he asked, glancing at his watch. It was nearly nine and if they got a solid three hours of work in, he could make the short trip into town and do a spot check at Pasco's, Franschhoek and see what was happening there. He'd noticed an upturn in expenses and a downturn in income and he needed to get to the bottom of that problem.

God, it never stopped.

Aisha linked her fingers together and rested her hands on her desk. 'No.'

Okay. 'When will you be ready? In ten minutes? Fifteen?'

Aisha turned her computer screen towards him, and he pulled his eyes off her lovely face to look at what he presumed to be an online appointment schedule. Aisha jabbed a finger at a red block from yesterday. 'I blocked off that time for you, yesterday. I have a slew of appointments this morning.'

Oh, crap. She was mad at *him*.

'I'm sorry I couldn't be here yesterday, but something came up. Can you not postpone this morning's appointments?'

Aisha scowled at him. 'I could, but I don't intend to.'

Young Aisha would've jumped to do as he asked; Aisha today wasn't budging. Dammit.

'Had you let me know earlier, I would've rearranged my schedule. But you didn't because your time is so much more important than mine.'

'Ro's restaurant is still in a planning phase. My restaurants are not. And if there's a problem, I need to put them first.' He wasn't being unreasonable, was he?

Aisha scanned her screen. 'We can get together tomorrow at four or Thursday at eleven,' she said in a very even, flat voice. He wasn't stupid enough to believe she wasn't still furious with him.

Pasco stood up and walked around to stand behind her. He looked at the appointments on her screen for the next few hours. He silently cursed when he saw she was scheduled to walk the grounds with St Urban's grounds manager. Her second appointment was with a local supplier of cleaning materials and housekeeping consumables and, because they'd want St Urban business, they'd be happy to reschedule.

'I'm sorry, it was rude of me not to give you more notice about my change of plans,' he said, half sitting on the edge of her desk. He nodded to the screen. He was running out of time, and he did need to get to Pasco's, Franschhoek today. 'Why don't you call those people, reschedule and let's get some real work done?'

Aisha stared at him for a minute, maybe longer, and it slowly dawned on Pasco he'd somehow made a bad situation a hundred times worse. How, he wasn't quite sure, but he had.

It was in her eyes, flashing *Abort! Danger ahead!* and in her flattened lips and tense jaw. She pushed her chair back and stood up, pushing back her light jacket to rest her hands on her curvy hips. He'd stroked those curves, kissed the smooth skin above her hip bone, slid his hands around to her truly spectacular butt.

'You arrogant, opinionated ass!'

He wasn't sure what surprised him more, her insult or her raised voice. He couldn't remember Aisha ever yelling before, didn't think she had it in her. During their marriage, she'd always been so even keeled, happy to acquiesce. Occasionally, he'd wished she'd stand up for herself more, but because he didn't have time for arguments, he'd appreciated her willingness to go with the flow. Kitchens were full of drama. He hadn't needed it at home too.

'How dare you stride in here and demand that I rearrange my working day to accommodate you? You might not respect my career—'

Whoa, hold on! 'Of course I respect your career!' he interrupted, standing to face her.

'If you did, you wouldn't have blown me off or sent me a message an hour after we were supposed to meet!'

She waved her hands in a shooing motion, trying to dismiss him. 'It doesn't matter.'

'Actually, it *does* matter. Don't shut down, *talk* to me.'

Her eyes widened at his statement, and she finally nodded. Frowning, she speared her hands into her hair.

'The bottom line is that you don't respect me, my time, or what I'm trying to do here! If you did, you wouldn't walk into my office looking for me to fall into line with your schedule, your wishes.'

Pasco winced. Okay, maybe he'd been a little heavy-handed in insisting she blow off her other appointments to be with him. Because that was what he wanted, her with him. He'd missed her, missed her smile and her voice, missed her in his bed. Missed her scent in his nose, and her body in his arms. His apartment felt empty without her.

'I was needed at The Vane,' Pasco carefully replied. 'My chef—'

'Of *course* you have to put the restaurant first. Your time is so much more valuable than *mine*. Guess that hasn't changed.'

He heard the bitterness in her voice and, worse, the derision. It pierced him with all the accuracy of a scalpel blade.

'Next time give me ample warning you can't make a meeting. I'm not someone who will wait around for you, Kildare. Respect me and respect my time.'

She brushed past him to cross the room to yank open the door to her office. 'When would you like to meet? Tomorrow at four or Thursday at eleven?' she demanded, gesturing for him to leave.

He saw the militant look in her eyes and internally winced. Knowing there was little point in arguing, and no chance of her changing her mind, he jammed his hands into the pockets of his chinos and walked towards her.

As for another meeting with her, that depended on what he found at Pasco's, Franschhoek today and tonight. 'I'll let you know,' he told her.

She lifted her chin. 'Fine,' she said through gritted teeth.

Pasco sighed, stopped and turned to face her. She was right, he'd been disrespectful today and she was right to call him out. If he wanted to have Aisha in his life, he'd have to do better, think more, stop believing he was the reason the world turned.

He'd been on his own for a long time and was the lord of his little fiefdom. Thanks to his power and success, people kowtowed to him, and he'd become spoiled.

Hell, even if Aisha weren't a factor, this facet of his life, of himself, could certainly do with a great deal of work.

'I really am sorry, sweetheart.'

He saw the surprise in her eyes at his genuine apology, but instead of inviting him back into her office, she slammed the door in his face.

And his respect for her inched upwards.

CHAPTER NINE

THROUGHOUT THE REST of her day, Aisha questioned her reaction to Pasco's lack of consideration, wondering if she'd allowed their past to colour her response to his actions. After all, rescheduling appointments was something she often did, and there had been many times when she couldn't make an appointment because something else arose. It was never a big deal.

But she always had the decency to let the other party know, to explain her actions. No, she decided, Kildare had messed up and she'd been right to let him know he was out of line. And, yes, maybe she had been a little ruder to him than necessary because she felt as if she'd been snapped back into the past and she was nineteen again, pacing their flat because he'd promised to come home early so that they could catch a late dinner. Or she was waiting in the hallway, her packed suitcase at her feet, waiting for him to take her on a weekend away only to find out, hours later, that he had to work. Alone in her bed, crying herself to sleep, because she was so damn lonely and felt neglected and unloved.

But she wasn't nineteen any more and she was a professional woman who stood up for herself.

You are so much stronger than the girl you were, Aisha, and you're not a pushover.

She grinned into the darkness. She'd come a long way.

Aisha scowled at the dark trees as she walked back to her cottage, navigating the path by the torch on her phone.

Tired and headachy, she pulled the pins out of her hair and allowed it to tumble down her back. She shoved the pins into the pocket of her jacket, hunching her shoulders against the cold wind cutting through her clothes. While she'd been nursing her anger at Pasco, a cold front had come in, bringing cloudy skies threatening rain, and a biting wind. She increased her pace, thinking about what she could eat when she got home. She tried to recall what was in her fridge and pulled a face. Apart from a few bottles of wine in her small wine rack—she'd be having a glass or three tonight—there wasn't much in her house in the way of food. She kept meaning to go into the village to stock up, but it kept getting shoved down to the bottom of her to-do list.

Maybe if she headed into town around lunchtime tomorrow, she could catch Pasco at his Franschhoek restaurant, nail down a time for them to meet and pick up some food, either before or after. And when they met again, they needed to have a tension-free, productive conversation about the restaurant. She had to get their working relationship back on track and, to do that, she'd have to keep her distance from him, to put space between them.

When he'd walked into her office earlier, her heart had fizzed and fumbled, stuttered, and stumbled. No man, before and after him, had ever made her feel off balance, shaky, as if she were attached to the charging pads of a defibrillator. Despite being incandescently angry with him, she'd had to grip the edge of her desk to stop herself from leaping into his arms.

His arms were where she most wanted to be. Dammit.

She couldn't regret sleeping with him—their lovemaking had been off-the-charts wonderful and she'd enjoyed every minute out of bed too—but she knew it couldn't happen again. Every non-professional encounter she had with him made her want more, encouraged her to throw caution to the wind, allowed him to slip a little deeper under her skin, a little further into her soul.

There was no future for them. There couldn't

be. He couldn't see her as an equal partner, would never make her a priority, and she could never settle for anything less.

Friends and fellow professionals, colleagues. That was all they could be.

Aisha walked up to her veranda and yelped when she saw a shadow-like figure in the corner. Then, when her mouth caught up to her brain, she let out a small screech and started to kick off her heels so she could bolt away.

'It's me, sweetheart,' Pasco said, not moving from his seat on the swing in the corner.

Aisha, off balance because she was only wearing one heel, slapped her hand to her chest and released a low growl. 'You scared me, Kildare! What the hell are you doing lurking on my veranda?'

'Waiting for you,' Pasco stated.

Looking down, Aisha located her heel and bent down to pick it up. Standing on one foot, she put her heel back on before stepping onto her veranda. Her eyes flicked over Pasco, noticing he'd pulled on a leather bomber jacket over his shirt and that his hair looked more messy than normal. In fact, he looked exhausted and, she squinted at him in the low light, sad.

'Everything okay, Pasco?' she asked him as she inserted her key into the lock before pushing open the door to her cottage.

'It's after eleven. Do you always work so late?' Pasco asked from a couple of steps behind her. 'Please tell me that my idiocy today isn't the reason you are home late.'

He looked genuinely contrite, so Aisha shook her head. 'No, this is my life.' Aisha dropped her laptop bag onto the dining table and watched him as he strode into her place, holding a large cooler box with ease.

'Got any wine?' he asked. He lifted the box with one hand. 'I'll trade a massive glass for lemon chicken, roasted potatoes with rosemary, roasted vegetables, and a pecan nut pie.'

Exhausted, she thought about asking him to leave, but her stomach was grumbling and she needed food. Then she looked at Pasco, really looked, and saw his tight lips, his turbulent expression, and the devastation in his eyes.

He looked both gutted and furious, upset and disheartened. Something had happened between him leaving her office and now, something that rocked his world.

'Sit down, Pasco,' she told him, kicking off her heels. Reaching for a bottle of red from her wine rack, she put it on the table and rooted around in a drawer to find the corkscrew. 'Open that and pour us some. The glasses are in the cupboard above the fridge. I'm just going to change into something warmer and more comfortable.'

Without replying, Pasco reached for the wine and Aisha scampered into her bedroom to change into a pair of track pants and an oversized hoodie. She pulled thick socks onto her feet and roughly pulled her hair back into a messy tail.

Aisha sighed as she caught a glimpse of herself in the freestanding mirror in the corner of her room. She looked about sixteen, and sloppy. But this wasn't a date. This was a meal—thank God!—some wine, and then she would send Pasco on his way.

What was he doing here anyway? Had he come to apologise?

Aisha walked back into the open-plan living area and saw that Pasco had not only poured wine, but was also in the process of unwrapping a plate of food. He tested the temperature with the back of his hand, grimaced, and stomped over to the microwave. Aisha had no problem heating food, but Pasco, picky chef that he was, despised the practice.

'Where's yours?' she asked, pulling out a chair and sitting down.

'I ate at the restaurant earlier,' Pasco replied, hitting buttons on the microwave.

He turned and his eyes slammed into hers and electricity—or annoyance, who could tell?—arced between them. He started to speak, but stopped when the microwave dinged. He turned, pulled the plate out, and placed it on the navy placemat in front of her. She breathed in the delicious smells of lemon, lemongrass and garlic, rosemary, and roasted chicken. Heaven, she thought, picking up her cutlery and digging in.

After five minutes of eating, she looked up to see Pasco still standing in front of the counter, his untouched wine glass next to him. He looked broody, tired, and as if he was about to snap.

'While I appreciate the food, I'm still not sure why you are here, Pasco,' Aisha stated.

'But thank you for bringing me food, it's delicious,' she added.

'It was one of the trainee chefs' chance to cook the staff meal at the restaurant. I think he did a decent job.'

More than decent, Aisha thought as she took another bite of chicken. Chewing, she watched as Pasco turned to stare out her kitchen window, wondering what he was looking at as it was pitch-black outside. His shoulders were tight with tension, and he kept massaging his neck, as if he was trying to rub away a knot in his muscles.

'Pas, come sit down,' Aisha told him. He turned to look at her over his shoulder, as if debating whether that was what he wanted to do, before nodding. He yanked out a chair and extended his long legs, crossing his feet at the ankles.

'Again, I am sorry about earlier. I was a jerk.'

'Accepted. So what happened today?'

Pasco leaned back, picked up his glass of wine, and downed it in one swallow. After refilling his glass, he looked at her, his gaze broody. 'My gut has been telling me that there's something wrong at my restaurant in Franschhoek for a while, but I ignored my instincts. Expenses are up, revenue is down, and I've been meaning to get there to find out what's going on, but I've been busy.'

'Couldn't your accountant or business manager investigate for you?' Aisha asked, taking her last bite and placing her cutlery together. 'That was fantastic, thank you. I was so hungry.'

'I could tell,' Pasco said, humour flashing in his eyes. 'That was a man-sized portion. Where do you put it all?'

'Fast metabolism,' Aisha told him. 'The restaurant?'

'My business manager and accountant both told me not to worry about it, that the margins were in the appropriate range and that it was probably just a temporary dip. Nothing to worry about because the manager is also one of my most trusted employees. Jason has been with me from the beginning. We worked together at my first restaurant in London.'

Aisha picked up her wine glass and took a sip, leaning back in her chair.

'When you kicked me out of your office—' Aisha started to protest, realised it was a fair statement, and nodded, refusing to feel guilty. He'd deserved it. But because she didn't believe in holding grudges, she gestured for him to continue.

'I headed over there. I was early, the only one there so I let myself in. I went straight to the office, thinking that I'd do a couple of spot checks. I was about to start when I heard a knock on the back door, the door where the staff enters.'

'Who was at the door, Pas?' Aisha asked when he hesitated.

Pasco rubbed his forehead with his fingers. 'Jason's wife. She had one baby in a pram, another on her hip and I could tell she'd been crying for what looked like days. She asked me if Jason was in, I told her no and her knees buckled, just for an instant. The baby started to wail, the toddler started screaming and it was pandemonium.'

'What did you do?'

'I invited her inside, gave her some coffee. After what seemed like hours, I got the story from her,' Pasco said, his expression bleak.

'And it wasn't pretty,' Aisha stated.

'Jason left her a couple of months ago and hasn't paid her any child support. She's all but destitute. She's being evicted and she came to see him. She needed money to go to her mother in Kimberley.'

'And Jason?' Aisha asked.

Pasco's gaze hardened. 'Well, apparently Jason has a new woman, a new house, and is spending every cent he earns, and that's a lot, on his new girlfriend. He's bought a new car, new clothes for her, furniture, jewellery. All this while his wife can't get any money from him to pay for nappies, formula, and the rent.'

Aisha winced, immediately angry. 'What a dirtbag.'

'Yeah,' Pasco replied. 'But he's a dirtbag I considered to be my friend. I don't recognise this, recognise him. That's not the guy I know.'

'That's the guy he's being right now,' Aisha told him. 'I presume you gave the wife a wad of cash?'

Pasco nodded. 'I arranged a driver to take her to Kimberley, paid her rent, and gave her money to buy what she needed,' Pasco said, in his furious, growly voice. 'Today was his day off and, in between helping out in the kitchen, I did some spot checks and he's been stealing from me.

'When he comes in tomorrow, I'm going to fire his ass,' Pasco told her.

'Do you have proof?'

'There are some dubious invoices that don't

look genuine. I think he's also been double-dipping.'

'Double-dipping?'

'He's claimed cash from petty cash on invoices that were paid on the company credit card. I'll bring in a team of forensic accountants to go through every scrap of paper.'

Aisha rubbed her thumb across his knuckles. 'I'm sorry he hurt you, Pas,' she quietly stated.

Pasco stared at her with haunted eyes. 'He was my first employee, Aish, he's been with me for years. Why do the people closest to you always let you down?'

He wasn't talking about Jason any more, and Aisha knew that the ghosts from the past had their cold fingers around his throat. 'You're thinking about your dad.'

He shrugged. 'How can I not? It's pretty much the same thing he did.'

No, Jason had opened up Pasco's wounds, he hadn't caused them. 'Tell me about your dad, Pas.'

Pasco jammed his thumb and index finger into his eye sockets and rubbed them, as if trying to dispel the memories. But when he looked up, Aisha saw that they were still swirling in his eyes.

'My mum tried hard to make her marriage work, but having her house repossessed was the last straw. We moved to Franschhoek, and my father stayed in the city. It was a tough, tough time. I remember listening to her crying herself to sleep. It didn't help that he wouldn't stop calling her or trying to see us, rocking up at midnight or four in the morning, causing scene after scene and threatening to take us away.

'Mum got a restraining order and instigated divorce proceedings. Then she went to work and put her head down to clear the debts he ran up in her name. She met John, my stepdad, but she refused to accept any financial help from anyone, including her wealthy family. She said she'd been the idiot, so she'd pay the price. We had some visits with him—they were awful because he wasn't that interested in us, he just ranted about my mum most of the time, constantly telling us how he was going to take us away,' Pasco explained. 'Then he dropped off the radar and I was hurt. Confused. And worried. And I felt guilty because John was around and he was great, stable, and interested in us, you know?'

Aisha nodded.

'I white-knuckled it through my last year of primary school, knowing that I was going to Duncan House. My grandfather and uncles all went to the school and my grandfather left money for the fees. That was what got me through that year, the knowledge that I was going to this fantastic school.'

Aisha sucked in a breath, suspecting what he was about to say next. 'A couple of weeks before I was due to start, my mum got a call from the school, asking for a meeting. She went in and when she came out, she was crying...'

Pasco's Adam's apple bobbed.

'Your dad stole that money too?' Aisha gently asked.

He stared out of the window, misery in his eyes. 'My mum, naively, believed he wouldn't stoop so low to take our education fund. But he had that damn power of attorney, and he did. My mum just shrank in on herself, fell apart. She handled losing her house, her savings, but losing the ability to fund her boys' education? That nearly killed her.'

'But you did go to Duncan House,' she pointed out. 'How did that happen?'

He smiled softly. 'After a week of watching my mum cry, John said to hell with it and he went to Duncan House and cut a cheque for both my and Cam's education, for the full five years each. My mum told him to cancel the cheque, that it wasn't his problem, and he told her he didn't have any kids, that he was going to marry her and he had pots of money. He told her he understood her desire to pay off his debts, but we were going to Duncan House and that was the end of it.'

'You must've been so relieved,' Aisha stated.

'Yeah, I was, but I was so pissed off with my father too,' Pasco replied, rubbing the back of his neck. 'I needed to talk to him, to confront him, you know?'

'Did you?'

Pasco nodded. 'I found out where he was living, I don't remember how, and I hitched a lift to the city and went to see him.'

'Go on, Pas,' Aisha said when he hesitated.

'I went to his apartment—God, that's too good a word for the hovel he was living in. I expected a house, something great to show for all the money he stole, but it was a hovel. There was a mattress on the floor, a sleeping bag, and a two-ring stove. No fridge. He said he lost the money in some pyramid scheme, and he was destitute. He asked *me* for money, his twelve-year-old son.

'I just stood there, wondering who the hell he was and how he could make such stupid decisions. I vowed I would never be like him, that I would be the exact opposite.'

A bankload of pennies dropped. That was why he was so driven, so committed to his career. Pasco's need to be successful was his way to heal the psychological wounds his father had inflicted. Aisha stared at him, feeling shocked and sad. 'What did you do?'

'Bolted out of there and called John. He collected me in the city and brought me home.'

Aisha stroked the back of his hand with the tips of her fingers. 'I'm sorry you had to go through that and I'm sorry Jason let you down and yanked all those old memories up again.'

'I don't understand how Jason can walk away from his family without looking back, how he can pretend they don't exist. I've done everything I can to make sure my family is financially secure. They'd never have to work a day in their lives again if they chose not to.'

Aisha tipped her head to the side. 'What do you mean?'

'There's a trust…if my parents or my brother, you, get into financial trouble, there's a massive trust with millions in it as a backup plan.'

'Me?' Aisha squeaked. 'Why am I there?'

He shrugged. 'I started the trust when we first married. Every cent I earned working overtime went into it.' He frowned at her. 'Why do you think I worked all those extra hours? I needed to make sure that you would be okay.'

Aisha buried her head in her hands and shook her head. 'God, Pasco!'

She hadn't needed a saviour or a financial backup plan, she'd needed her husband. She'd needed his time and attention and that was why she'd walked. Yet, because he'd been so disappointed by his father, he went to the other extreme to be the exact opposite. And their marriage fell apart because they were useless at communicating.

His previous actions suddenly made so much more sense to her than they ever did before. He'd become a workaholic, someone who couldn't sit still for more than a second. He needed to work because if he took a minute to relax, he thought he was becoming like his dad, and he couldn't bear the thought.

Pasco was hard-wired to give his businesses everything he had. She now understood his need to succeed, his determination and his drive. It wasn't because he was ruthlessly ambitious, but because he needed to protect the ones he loved, to plot and plan so that he would never let anyone down the way his dad did him.

She understood his impulse to make sure everyone's ducks were in a row, but that wasn't his job. She most certainly didn't need the money in his trust, for him to be her backup plan. How to say this, frame this, without getting his back up?

'Pas, you are not responsible for the actions of others, and it's not your job to clean up your dad's mess.'

'He stole my mum's money…' Pasco hotly replied.

'Yeah, he did.' Aisha took a deep breath,

knowing what she was about to say would be hard for him to hear. 'But your mum played a part in letting that happen. And, judging by what you said about her repaying her own debts, she's owned her actions and has accepted her part in the fiasco.

'Your stepfather is rich, your brother is financially stable, I'm fine…none of us *needs* you to be our backup plan, Pasco. You are not responsible for our financial well-being. We have to be able to stand and fall by our own decisions. *Our* choices, *our* consequences.'

He stared at her, turmoil in his eyes. She pointed a finger at him. 'Stop trying to control the world, Pas. Let the people you love, who love you, be your partners and not your responsibility.'

Something flashed in his eyes, an emotion she couldn't identify. She could see he wanted to argue but it was late and she was tired, and she'd given him enough to think of for now.

He'd either see it her way, or he wouldn't…she couldn't impose her beliefs on him.

Aisha stood up, walked around the table, and slung her thigh over Pasco's. He pulled his knees up, his hands instinctively going to her hips. Aisha brushed his hair back from his face and slowly lowered her head, allowing her breasts to sink into his hard chest. Her mouth touched his and she gently nibbled his lower lip. She was mentally exhausted and he, she assumed, was too. It was time to put this day behind them, to relax and recharge. And she knew a very good way to do that.

'Think about what I said. But only much, much later.'

CHAPTER TEN

SERVICE FOR THE Tempest-Vane ball had been a bitch and Pasco was running an hour later than he expected. After a quick shower, he pulled on his black suit, white shirt, and black tie—nothing showy—and headed to the ballroom on the third floor, directly above his busy restaurant. He hesitated, thinking he should check in with his restaurant staff, but knew that if he did he'd be sucked into whatever was happening in the kitchen.

Nobody had called him with an issue, so he'd just let sleeping restaurant dogs lie.

And…he really couldn't wait to get to the ball to see Aisha.

Something had changed since their conversation about his dad at her cottage, and their connection had, despite their busy schedules, deepened. He'd spent a lot of time thinking about what she'd said about his need to be responsible for everyone and everything and thought she had a point. But how to change the habits of a lifetime was still giving him trouble. Being protective was wired into his DNA and he didn't know if he'd ever stop worrying about the people he loved.

Pasco stepped into the lift, his blood fizzing with anticipation at seeing his lover. The past few weeks had been incredibly busy, but they'd managed, somehow, to have a few arrive-late-and-leave-early sleepovers. When they couldn't be together, their early-morning and late-night phone calls got him through the hours until they could be together again.

Their busy lives weren't ideal, but they were making it work, trying to accommodate each other as much and whenever they could. They were certainly communicating better and their lovemaking was…yeah, bloody fantastic. Better than it had ever been.

But he still felt dissatisfied and wanted more. More time, more making love, more conversations about everything and nothing.

More.

It was strange to feel like this and Pasco wasn't sure how to cope with his restlessness. Ten years ago, five, working like a demon got his blood pumping, made him feel ten feet tall. Now all he felt was frustrated. And tired.

The last month had been a perfect storm, with

Hank bombarding him with videos of a warehouse space he was convinced would make an awesome restaurant and entreaties to come back to the States. His producers wanted a definite answer on whether he was going to do another season of his popular travel show and he was dashing between The Vane, dropping in on St Urban before heading to Pasco's, Franschhoek, where he'd installed a temporary chef and manager.

He hadn't visited Binta for a few weeks and he was also neglecting his kitchenware line. Frankly, all he wanted to do was ignore all of it and spend some time with Aisha, have a leisurely meal, catch a movie, watch the sun go down behind the Simonsberg mountain with a glass of red in his hand and her at his side.

Maybe a dog lying at his feet.

Pasco rubbed his face, surprised by his longing for domesticity. But there was only one woman he could see as his wife and that was his ex-wife.

Did he really want to do that? Go there? Or was he just overworked and tired? Stressed? But a little voice inside him insisted that his first choice was the only woman with whom he could imagine spending the rest of his life.

Absurd notion—preposterous, really—but it didn't make it any less true. Aisha was it for him.

But they'd tried once, and they'd failed. How

could they—even if she was interested in trying again—be together? Aisha was up for a promotion and if she got it, and she would because she was bloody brilliant at her job, she had the option to live in London or Johannesburg. If she moved to London and he didn't move back to New York, they'd only, with their schedules, occasionally see each other.

But seeing each other when they could was better than nothing. But he knew, after a few months of incessant travelling, the novelty would quickly fade, and travelling would become a drag. And, in time, they'd drift apart.

Crap, he simply couldn't find a solution.

Living apart was not what he wanted anyway. He wanted to see Aisha every day, in every light, and in every way. He wanted her in his bed, on his deck when he woke up, to meet her for lunch or an afternoon quickie. He wanted a life with her, he wanted a *wife*.

But to get what he wanted, one of them would have to make a massive sacrifice. He would either have to slow down, or Aisha would have to give up her job. Neither option was possible.

He couldn't slow down; he'd tried that before and he'd been miserable. Aisha had worked damn hard for her promotion, and he couldn't ask her to give that up—that wouldn't be fair.

Devil, meet Deep Blue Sea.

Why did relationships have to be so damn complicated? This was why he'd avoided them for so long: he didn't like thinking this hard. Oh, and he probably also avoided relationships with other women because he was still in love with his wife.

He'd never stopped being in love with her.

Pasco stepped into the lavishly decorated ballroom—white and gold—searching for Aisha in the sea of black-and-white tuxedos and ball gowns. Navy blue seemed to be the favoured colour this year, along with a dark, turbulent grey.

Pasco caught a flash of dazzling, deep pink and sucked in a breath. Stepping to the side, he saw Aisha standing next to the dance floor, talking to Muzi. She wore a ruffled sari, the fuchsia colour eye-popping. A heavily jewel-embellished, teeny-tiny blouse and matching belt gave her traditional outfit a trendy vibe.

And yeah, he loved the deep vee in her blouse hinting at her stunning breasts and, because she had a drool-worthy body, the way the dress highlighted her tiny waist and stunning skin.

Pasco forced his feet to move and when he reached her, he took in the matching colour of her lipstick, her subtle make-up, and the tiny silver bindi placed between her eyebrows. She'd straightened her hair and it fell in a thick black fall of shine down her back.

She looked sensational…strip-her-down-and-take-her-to-bed stunning.

Aisha's blush, Muzi's deep laugh, and Aisha's elbow in his ribs told him he'd said that last sentence out aloud. Oh, well, it was the truth.

Pasco shook Muzi's hand and pulled his friend in for a quick, manly hug. 'How's Ro?' Pasco asked.

'Hanging in there.' Muzi grimaced.

'She's done well to keep those babies in as long as she has,' Aisha told Muzi.

'Yeah.' Muzi pulled back his jacket sleeve to look at his watch. 'It's getting late. I'm off.'

Pasco clasped his shoulder. 'Let us know if anything happens baby-wise.'

'Will do,' Muzi said before striding away.

Aisha sent him a quick smile. 'He's a basket case.'

'He adores Ro and is worried about her,' Pasco replied, watching his friend's progress across the room.

Aisha took a champagne glass from a waiter holding a tray and Pasco ordered a bourbon. She sipped and let her eyes drift across the room. 'Do you want kids?' she asked.

He wasn't completely surprised by her question. He'd seen the longing in her eyes when she eyed Ro's ginormous stomach. 'I haven't given it much thought. But if I did, I'd only want to have them with you.'

Aisha stared at him, shocked. 'What?'

'You heard me,' Pasco replied, jamming his hands into the pockets of his suit trousers.

'But you and I, we're just—' Aisha stumbled over her words and her glass wobbled. He plucked it from her fingers and placed it on a high table and linked her fingers in his.

He dropped his head and placed a kiss on her temple, breathing in her feminine, lovely, too-sexy scent. 'Lovers? Exes? Friends? We're all of that, but we're also so much more.'

'How much more, Pas?' Aisha asked him, her eyes wide with surprise.

Pasco took her hand, pulled her to the dance floor and into his arms. He rested his cheek against the side of her head as they glided around the floor. Their bodies, as always, were completely in sync, and they moved easily together.

'I think we should discuss that, discuss us,' Pasco told her, wincing at the tremble he heard in his voice. Damn, but he was nervous. 'Would rewriting the rules be something you'd be interested in doing?'

He held his breath, scared she'd say no. His heart slowed down, and he forgot to breathe.

'Yes.'

There it was, thank *God*. He released the tension in his shoulders, in his spine, and closed his eyes in relief. 'Can I take you to dinner next Saturday night, somewhere wildly romantic? Maybe we can figure something out, to see if we can get from here to…babies.'

She didn't reply, and Pas could feel tension running through her. He pulled back to look at her, saw her eyes fill with emotion. He couldn't decide whether fear or excitement had the upper hand, but he intended to find out. 'Is that something you want, sweetheart?'

'I don't know what I want, Pas. And feeling like this again scares me,' Aisha softly replied, resting her head against his chest.

'I know, I'm scared too. But maybe we can figure it out together,' Pasco murmured, before pulling her closer and holding her tighter.

Late on Wednesday afternoon, Aisha sat in her office, sifting through résumés of people applying for the top positions at St Urban—permanent hotel manager, chef, food, and beverage manager—but after reading the same résumé twice, she pushed the folders aside, and her chair back, and captured her hands between her knees, frustrated by her inability to concentrate.

Pasco wanted to talk about their relationship. God, she was in a relationship with her ex-husband… How did that happen?

That had been rule number one, do not fall for your ex, and she'd broken it a hundred times over. What was she thinking? Had she been thinking at all? No, as it had years before, her brain shut down whenever she came within six feet of the man!

Aisha bit her bottom lip and stared at her shoes. She appreciated him wanting to find a way for them to be together, but this time around, she was trying to be sensible, to think things through. She was going to be in the country for another four, maybe five months, and if she got the promotion, she'd have to decide on moving to Johannesburg or London. If she wasn't promoted, she'd be moving on to the next project, which could be in Canada or Cartagena.

Either way, she'd be hours and hours away from Pasco. And yes, she understood that some people managed to make long-distance relationships work, but she didn't see how they could. They couldn't even make it work when they'd lived together in the same apartment.

Yes, they were older and more mature, but realistically, they were already struggling to carve out time to spend together. How would they manage that when they were in different cities, different time zones?

She wanted to be with him, see more of him, but...how?

Her computer indicated she had a video call and, happy to be distracted from her thoughts, which were going around and around, Aisha pounced on it, wincing when she saw it was her mum calling. Unable to cut the call, she rubbed her fingers across her forehead and sighed. 'Hi, Mum.'

'I'm phoning to see if you are coming to dinner, not this Saturday but the next. Everybody will be there.'

Would it hurt her mum, just once, to open a conversation with a *'Hello, darling, how are you?'*?

'I don't think so, Mum.'

'Why not?'

Oh, let me count the reasons.

'Because you all but ignored me at Oscar's party and when I did speak, my opinion was instantly dismissed? Because the family spoke over and interrupted me?'

'We don't do that!'

Oh, enough now! She'd always been careful to dance around her mum's feelings, but she didn't have the time or the energy to massage her mum's delicate ego. Or anyone else's! She was done with bottling up her emotions to make people feel comfortable. 'Mum, what's the point? Really?'

'You're our daughter—'

'Well, it doesn't feel like it! Growing up I felt like the ugly stepchild, never part of the family, and nothing has changed.'

'We don't—'

She sounded a little mortified, but Aisha was past caring. This moment had been a long time in coming. 'Mum, I get it, you're all intellectuals and I don't fit in. I don't get advanced maths or know how to map the neural pathways of the brain. But I'm not an idiot!'

'Well, none of us think you are.'

Aisha scoffed at her tepid response. Really? That was news to her. 'I don't fit into the family, Mum. I never have.'

It felt good to verbalise her long-held hurts, to tell her mother how she felt. It felt a little like poison leaving her system, as if her blood were thinner, her heart able to beat a fraction better.

'That's not true!'

Aisha sighed. 'It's true for me, Mum.'

'If that's how you feel,' her mum stated, her voice stiff with outrage, 'I'm not going to beg you to change your mind.'

'Mum, don't be like that, okay? Everything is fixable, but only if we communicate and compromise. Talk to Dad and give me a call in a day or two if you think we can find another way of dealing with each other. Maybe, instead of a family dinner, it could just be the three of us. What do you think?'

'I'll talk to your father,' her mum muttered.

Honestly, that was more progress than she'd expected.

Aisha lowered her phone, saw the call had been dropped and rested her forehead on her desk. Look at her, taking names and kicking butt! Aisha hauled in a deep breath, feeling lighter and brighter. She was learning about boundaries and what she would and wouldn't accept. She was making others, and herself, take responsibility for their actions and behaviours. She was finally learning to take care of herself.

And damn, it felt good.

Aisha heard the beep of an incoming video call coming in on her computer, pushed her hand through her hair and faced her screen, her hand clicking her wireless mouse.

Her boss's lovely face appeared on her screen and her white teeth flashed as she smiled. Aisha sighed, relieved.

'Hello, Miles,' Aisha said, leaning forward. Thank God for work, the one thing in her life that wasn't complicated.

Miles's smile faded and she leaned forward, her expression concerned. 'Damn, girl, you look like hell! How hard are you working? Are you sleeping?'

Miles, under her sleek and sophisticated facade, was a bit of a mother duck. 'Lots to do, Miles.'

'How's the restaurant coming on?' Miles asked.

Slowly, because she and Pasco often got distracted. But they'd get it done. She wouldn't let down Ro. 'It's coming.'

'I know that I dumped that on you, Aisha,' Miles told her, wincing. 'But I don't want you killing yourself. If you can't manage, I'll send someone—maybe Kendall—to take over the establishment of the restaurant.'

Kendall was young, sexy, and an incorrigible flirt. She'd take one look at Pasco and decide to add him as a notch on her bedpost. Aisha had no problem with Kendall's relaxed attitude to men and sex—her body, her rules—but not when it involved her husband…dammit, her ex-husband.

Uh, no. She'd rather work her fingers to the bone, thank you very much.

'I'll let you know if I get overwhelmed, Miles,' she said through gritted teeth. No, she wouldn't.

'Your call,' Miles replied. 'So, I know it's late notice, but Dad and I are flying into Johannesburg tomorrow evening, and we want to have a strategy meeting all day Friday and Saturday morning. On Saturday night, Dad is hosting dinner at his house for senior management, and he wants you to join us.'

Getting an invite to the chairman of the board's house was a big deal, something that hadn't happened to her before. It wasn't a leap to believe she had a better than average chance of being promoted.

Aisha felt the buzz of excitement and told herself not to gush. 'That would be...' Oh, *crap*. Pasco. They'd made plans for Saturday night, and he'd pulled strings to get into a spectacular restaurant in Cape Town, a place where you had to wait months to get a reservation, and he wanted to talk.

'You have plans...' Miles stated. 'Hot date?'

Aisha scratched her forehead, not wanting to lie. 'Yes, but I'll cancel...'

'Judging by your torn expression, it sounds like meeting him is important to you.'

It was, but was it as important as her job? She wished she could say that it wasn't, but she couldn't. Equally important, maybe.

And that was the difference between her and Pasco: he didn't hesitate to put his work first. No, that wasn't fair, not any more. Pasco was definitely getting better at making her a priority. And how ironic was it she was the one who now had to choose between her man and her work? But she couldn't pass this invite up. Pasco would understand. 'Please thank your dad for the invite, and yes, I'll be there.'

To her consternation, Miles shook her head, her expression pensive. 'We'll be done with business by lunchtime Saturday. Book a flight back for mid-afternoon and you can still make your date.'

Aisha frowned. 'Really, it's fine, I'll cancel.'

'It's a casual dinner, Aisha, not a referendum on your work. And you know that I'm all about a work-play balance. You work too much and play too little so you're going on that date.'

'Your dad won't see it that way,' Aisha protested. Miles's father expected his employees to say, 'How high?' when he said, 'Jump'. She often thanked God that Miles and not her father was her boss—she would've resigned years ago. Aisha was also grateful that Mr Lintel would be retired when—*if*—she got the promotion.

'Aisha, I'm grateful for your work ethic, I really am. But I worry about your workaholic tendencies.'

She was a workaholic? She snorted. She was an amateur compared to Pasco.

'I worry about you because you don't worry about yourself enough. I'm the one who has to insist that you take a vacation, who practically has to force a pay rise on you. I'm thrilled that you are dating and even more thrilled this man is important to you.'

He was, unfortunately. Always had been, probably always would be.

'Is he based in Cape Town?'

'Yes,' Aisha muttered, wondering why Miles was asking.

'Is it serious?'

Miles wasn't going to let this go. Her boss was a bull terrier when she sank her teeth into something, so Aisha might as well admit the truth and save them some time. 'We were married when I was very young. We've recently reconnected and it's…complicated.'

Miles opened her mouth to speak, closed it again, her lips moving in a silent 'wow'. 'I did not know that.'

Few people did.

'He's a very busy guy, but he's taking me to Michel's on Saturday night to see if we can find a way forward.'

Miles whistled. 'Michel's? You lucky thing, I waited for ever to eat there. Right, that settles it, you're flying back Saturday afternoon.'

'Mr Lintel won't be happy—' Aisha protested.

'I'll handle my dad,' Miles informed her. 'Look, Dad isn't convinced that you are ready to be promoted but I am, Aisha. When I move up into the CEO position, I want you as my operations officer.'

She knew that Mr Lintel had his reservations,

but hearing her suspicions confirmed made Aisha wince. Maybe she should cancel on Pasco and go to that dinner.

'Don't even think about it,' Miles warned her. She lifted her finger to point it at her screen. 'You need a life and when you get the promotion, I will be pushing you to find more balance in your life. And if some mad-about-you man wants you to stay in Cape Town, we can make that happen. After Covid-19, we've all realised what can be achieved by working remotely.'

Aisha released a long sigh, a mixture of confusion, relief, and sadness. 'I appreciate that, Miles, I do. I just don't know if things will work out with Pasco. Our relationship has been anything but smooth sailing.'

'Relationships aren't supposed to go smoothly, Aisha. Where's the fun in that? They are supposed to have dips and highs, valleys and summits. How you navigate the obstacles is what matters, how you love each other through the hard times.'

Aisha lifted her eyebrows. 'Did you learn that from the Danish prince you're dating?'

'No, I learned that from watching my folks stay married for close to thirty-five years,' Miles replied.

'Right, that's sorted. I'll see you on Friday in Joburg, okay?'

'Okay.' Aisha glanced down at the pile of résumés on her desk. 'Can I ask you a quick question about St Urban and my search for a general manager…?'

'Sure, hit me.'

God, she loved her job. At least she knew what she was doing there.

Due to Jason's suspected malfeasance, Pasco was working at his restaurant in Franschhoek on Wednesday night and, thanks to the unexpected arrival of a tour bus of English tourists, he saw his plans for sneaking out early to spend the night with Aisha fading away. The tourists were in a mood to party, his kitchen was slammed, and the bartenders and waitresses were run off their feet.

Pasco found himself pulled a hundred directions and when he stepped into the restaurant from the kitchen, he saw Aisha sitting at the bar and pushed away a surge of irritation.

He wasn't irritated by her presence, but by the fact he hadn't seen her since the ball and, thanks to their busy schedules, knew that they wouldn't be able to spend some quality time together before Saturday night.

The freaking sky could fall in but nothing— repeat, *nothing*!—was going to interfere with his plans for Saturday night. And Sunday.

Pasco lifted a hand in her direction, spoke to a waitress, and sighed when one of his regulars stood up to speak to him. It took ten minutes for him to reach Aisha, which was about nine and half minutes too long.

Bending his head, he kissed her temple and wrapped his hand around her wrist. 'Come with me,' he told her.

Aisha followed him through the doors marked 'staff only' and down a short hallway that led to his office. Standing back, he urged her inside, followed her in, and slammed the door shut, twisting the lock. Not giving her time to speak, he lowered his lips to hers, taking her mouth in a need-you-now kiss.

Aisha, so responsive, opened her mouth to his insistent tongue, and he couldn't resist sliding his hand up and under her thin jersey to thumb her already responsive nipple. Why did they put work first when being together, loving each other, felt like this? What was wrong with them?

Pasco felt lust flash through him as she angled her head to allow him deeper access to her mouth, her tongue tangling with his. She moaned, a sexy sound deep in her throat, and dropped her hands from his shoulders to run her fingers across his stomach, letting them drift over his aching erection before settling them low on his narrow hips.

Three hard raps on the door had him lifting his head. 'Give me a goddamn minute!' he shouted.

He heard footsteps fading away and immediately returned to kissing Aisha. Seeing her was an unexpected pleasure and the rest of the world could give him five minutes. Or thirty. Or a couple of hours. What the hell could be so damn important?

Pasco nuzzled her neck and lifted her sweater to her collarbone, tonguing her breast through the lace fabric covering her nipple. He yanked her bra cup aside and took her nipple into his mouth, smiling when he felt her hand in his hair, holding him in place.

She loved what he did to her…and he loved doing it. Win-win. Caught up in the passion between them, he drank her in. Not able to resist, he slipped a hand between her legs to cup her.

'Pas!'

Pasco heard the need in her voice and fumbled with the zip to her jeans so that he could feel her hot flesh on his fingers.

Someone banged on the office door again. 'Boss?'

Pasco lifted his head from her mouth to glare at the door. 'What?' he shouted, annoyed.

'Uh…another bus of tourists has arrived. We need another pair of hands at the bar.'

Pasco groaned and rested his forehead against

Aisha's. He closed his eyes and pulled his hands up to rest them on her hips, quietly muttering a string of curse words.

'I just wanted a half hour with you,' he murmured, wrapping his arms around her. 'Thirty minutes, that was all.'

Aisha's hands rubbed his back. 'Bad timing.'

He pulled back to run a hand over her hair. 'Do we have any other type of timing?' he asked, sounding rueful. And a little pissed off.

'Seems not,' Aisha replied, pushing her hands into the back pockets of her jeans. 'And on that point, about Saturday night…'

Pasco saw the apology in her eyes and grimaced. 'You're cancelling our plans?'

He felt the wave of disappointment, a small stab somewhere in the region of his heart. Was this the way she felt every time he cancelled their plans before? Frankly, it sucked.

'Not cancelling, just amending,' Aisha replied.

Pasco released his pent-up breath, relieved. Aisha went on to explain she was leaving for Johannesburg for work and would be returning on the four o'clock flight Saturday afternoon. 'I should probably stay for the chairman's dinner—I was specifically invited—but I'm skipping out.'

For Aisha that was a big deal and he appreciated it. 'No problem. Shall I push the reservation back from seven to eight?' he asked.

'Yes, please.'

She rubbed the back of her neck and he noticed she looked tired. 'Would it help if I collected you from the airport?'

Aisha shook her head. 'No, don't worry. I'm leaving my car there, so I'll just meet you at your Fresnaye apartment. If I land at six, I can be there by half-seven, I imagine.'

She'd still want to shower, do her hair. 'I'll make the reservation for eight-thirty.'

'Thanks.' She glanced at the locked door and nodded. 'You should go, you're needed.'

He was, but he wanted to know why her eyes held a hint of worry, why the muscles in her neck were hard with tension. 'Everything okay?'

'Sure.' She looked away and Pasco knew she was lying, that she was worried about something. Him? Them? Their relationship? He didn't blame her; he also spent hours wondering whether they were doing the right thing by hurtling into something deeper, something that could drown them. He wasn't any closer to figuring out how they could be together without one of them reinventing their lives, something he wasn't able to do.

No, that wasn't true…he, mostly, didn't *want* to change his life. It was busy and demanding and exciting. He just wished it left a little more time for him to spend with Aisha. And, yeah, he wished that her schedule weren't quite so busy…

Hypocritical, Kildare? Sure.

Pasco heard a roar coming from the bar and knew he had to get back to work. Stepping around Aisha, he unlocked the door. 'I have to get back.'

Aisha nodded. 'Duty calls.'

He slid his mouth across hers and pulled back before he lost control again and told the rest of the world to go to hell. 'See you Saturday.' He ran his thumb across her bottom lip, not convinced she was fine.

Honestly, the weekend couldn't come soon enough.

CHAPTER ELEVEN

AISHA FIDDLED WITH the stem of her wine glass and fought the urge to look at her watch again. It was half-nine and she'd been sitting at this table in Michel's for the past forty-five minutes waiting for Pasco. She felt the inquisitive eyes of her waitress on her and knew that if she met her gaze, she'd see sympathy and curiosity on her face.

Sympathy because, yeah, she'd been stood up, curiosity because few people had the balls to miss a meal at Michel's.

Pasco was one of the few people who would.

Aisha ran her fingertips over her forehead, her elbow on the table. What a stupid, crazy, super-stressful day. The strategy session ran later than expected and she saw Mr Lintel's frown when she excused herself, not happy she was leaving early. When she ran into the domestic departure terminal, her name was being called on the public announcement system. She cleared check-in at speed and ran to her gate, apologising to the unimpressed attendants.

She found her seat on the plane, ignored the dirty looks she received at holding up the flight—*It was five minutes, people!*—and fastened her seat belt. She, and everyone else, expected to hear the engines start but nothing happened. Fifteen minutes later, she was told that the flight was delayed because another aircraft needed to land unexpectedly.

It wasn't an emergency, the air hostess told them over loud groans, but they were expecting a half-hour delay, which turned into forty-five minutes.

On hearing she would be landing in Cape Town later than expected, she called Pasco to give him an update, but he didn't answer his phone. She sent him an email, a text message, and a WhatsApp message, all of which he didn't respond to.

When she landed in Cape Town, she still hadn't heard from him and placed another call; this time his message went straight to voicemail. Unsure what to do—had he lost his phone? Was it dead?—she called Michel's and asked them whether he'd cancelled their reservation. He hadn't so she decided to head straight for the restaurant. Choosing to believe, fool that she was, that he'd be there.

She arrived at eight forty-five and he'd yet to contact her.

Was he hurt? Dead? What the hell was wrong with his phone that he couldn't call?

Aisha looked down at her white shirt, which looked a little limp and not so white any more. She'd bought a red cocktail dress for this occasion, gorgeous shoes, and had planned on curling her hair. She'd rushed from the airport to this fancy restaurant and, feeling limp and looking ragged—and sitting here alone—she stuck out like a sore thumb.

Dammit, Kildare, where the hell are you?

He'll be here, a little voice deep inside her responded, just give him more time.

She'd wait another ten minutes, not a minute more. Aisha took a sip of wine and looked out of the window to watch the waves breaking over the rocks below. The spotlight on the restaurant's roof illuminated the rocky seascape below and Aisha idly watched a crab scuttle across a rock, dodging an incoming wave.

That was how she felt about life with Pasco, as if she were constantly dodging rogue waves.

Aisha sighed. Why had she ignored her rule not to fall in love with him, to keep her emotional distance? When they first reunited, she knew she had to be careful, that he could upend her world again. But instead of setting out clear boundaries, obeying the rules, she'd fallen under his spell again.

Could she have been more of a fool?

Aisha watched as an older woman across the room pulled out a credit card to pay for her and her husband's meal. That was what she wanted, she thought, an equal partnership, give and take, to be able to make decisions with him. She wanted Pasco to respect her career and to support her in it.

And she wanted to spend time with him, eating the whole fruit basket instead of just taking bites of the apple now and again.

But the reality was that if they decided to take another chance on their relationship, and to make it work, one of them would have to slow down. Would Pasco expect her to cut back on her workload without changing his hours? Would she be the one to make the sacrifices, working twice as hard as he did to give their relationship a shot?

Look, she got it, she wasn't stupid. He was a hotshot chef with a billion-dollar empire to look after and that ate up his time. But to have a relationship, one of them would have to concede, to give more than the other, and Aisha knew it would be her.

And if she did that, how long would it take before she started to feel resentful, for her to start nagging him to spend more time with her? How long would it be before she left him again?

What would Pasco give up? If anything?

Aisha dumped some more red wine into her glass and scowled at the empty seat opposite her. Another five minutes had passed, and she'd heard crickets. There was no excuse for his behaviour.

He wasn't dead or hurt, he was probably just ignoring her calls because he'd got sucked into work—at The Vane, in Franschhoek, or at Binta—and he didn't want to deal with her annoyance and anger.

In the morning he'd rock up at her door and apologise, saying he got delayed or his phone died or some other stupid excuse, and he'd try to charm her into forgiving him. If words didn't work he'd kiss her, knowing she was putty in his hands. He'd take her to bed, hoping that some good sex would improve her mood.

To be fair, it normally did.

Aisha felt fury burn away the moisture in her eyes. She'd had a hell of a day, and she'd all but killed herself to make her flight, had driven like a madman to get to this restaurant. She'd left a work event, incurring the chairman of the board's displeasure at her leaving the strategy meeting early—something she wasn't too worried about because she had Miles's support—to make this date with Pasco...

And he'd bloody stood her up.

If she needed a clear message on how life with Pasco would be going forward, this was it, big and bold and written in sparkly, six-foot-high letters.

You are always going to be last on his list of priorities...

She'd been kidding herself to think that anything had changed, that Pasco had changed, that he was ready to make space for her in his life. He was as committed to his career as he always was, he'd shown that over and over again. She'd struggled to get him to pay attention to the pop-up restaurant and when she did make arrangements with him to meet, he stood her up. He'd told her, time and time again, that he decided on his priorities and that his work, and his business interests, came first.

She stood on the outside of his life, only welcome in when it suited him. And didn't that feel familiar? Wasn't that the way she felt with her family? And, God, why did she keep choosing to love people who made her feel unseen, neglected, and less than?

She had to stop that, had to break that cycle. She was worthy of a man who put her first, who moved heaven and earth to be with her. She deserved to be a priority, to be considered, to be seen… She deserved a man who would support her, who would respect her enough to send her a damn message when he couldn't make a date.

Enough!

Enough of waiting for him, hoping for him to change, hoping for more than Pasco was able to give. This stopped now, tonight. She was done with hoping and wishing…

It was time to face the truth. She loved Pasco, she did, but she didn't like feeling 'less than', unsupported, dismissed. She needed to be a priority in his life, to be an equal partner, to step into the inner circle of his life.

It wasn't going to happen, and it was time she accepted that. Yes, she loved him, probably always would, but love couldn't exist in a vacuum and sometimes it simply wasn't enough.

Aisha reached into her bag to pull out her purse and placed enough money under the side plate to cover the mostly full bottle of wine. She pushed her purse back into her bag and her heart went into freefall when she saw her screen light up, showing an unfamiliar number.

She jabbed her finger on the green button and held the device up to her ear.

'Aish? Sorry—'

Aisha heard a man shouting, was Pasco in a *pub*? His voice faded in and out—the signal was terrible—but she heard a 'sorry' and 'in the morning'.

Aisha didn't say anything, she just cut the call, stood up on shaky legs, and pulled her bag over her shoulder.

She'd made him a priority but, to him, she was still an option.

That stopped right now.

The fire at Pasco's, Franschhoek broke out in the late afternoon, shortly after he left Franschhoek to head back to the city for his date with Aisha. By the time Pasco arrived back in the village, the old cottage, with its wooden floors, door frames, and wooden furniture, was fully engulfed. The fire engine took its time getting there, and the firefighters found him, his brother, Cam, his staff and many Franschhoek residents trying to douse the flames with hosepipes and buckets of water.

Frankly, their efforts hadn't made any difference.

Pasco glanced at the mountain, bathed in the early-morning light as he walked the long route to Aisha's cottage after a night of no sleep.

He needed the time to think, to work out what he was going to say to her, how to apologise. After telling Aisha how important this date was, how much he was looking forward to finding a way forward, it had been hours before he thought to call her. On seeing the fire, he'd immediately gone into his solve-this-and-sort-it-out zone, not allowing himself to be distracted. He'd hauled hosepipes and buckets of water, manned the hose of the ancient fire engine, beat at the burning bushes with blankets. He'd comforted his shocked employees and driven those who used public transport home.

He'd had a building and a business to save, and nothing else, at that moment, was important. He'd inherited his ability to focus on one thing, to the exclusion of everything else, from his father, and it made him an incredible chef, perfectionistic and driven. It also made him a lousy human being.

It wasn't that he hadn't thought about her—he had, he'd just pushed the need to contact her away. Caught up with the fire and what he had to do, he'd decided she could wait. But it really wouldn't have taken much to run to his car and send her a message, a quick call…five minutes? Ten? But no, because he was a control freak, he couldn't step away for even that long. Something might happen, he might miss something, he might be needed… As a result, it was after nine before he called her and, although the signal had been terrible, he'd immediately sensed her anger and disappointment.

He'd let her down *again*.

Was he ever going to stop doing that? Was it even *possible*?

Feeling sick and sad, he let his thoughts drift from Aisha to his restaurant and the cause of the fire. He'd heard mutterings about old wiring starting the blaze, or a pan of oil being left on the stove. BS, all of it. He'd had the house completely rewired a couple of years ago and his staff followed protocols at the end of a shift, including the washing and packing away of all used pots and pans. The fryer was emptied of oil and power cut to all the equipment in the kitchen. He knew without a shadow of a doubt that all those protocols had been followed because he'd run the kitchen during the lunch service and he'd checked.

Pasco knocked on the door to Aisha's cottage and waited for her to answer the door. There was only one logical explanation for a fire that burned so hot and so fast and that was that it had had some help from an accelerant.

And there was only one person who was pissed off enough to do that to him. Jesus, Jason.

Aisha answered the door, dressed in a pair of men's style flannel pyjamas, her hair early-morning messy. She frowned at him.

'It's just past seven, Kildare. What are you doing here so early?' she asked, her tone cool and her expression closed off. 'Actually, you know what? I don't care. Just go away.'

Her reaction wasn't unexpected, but because she didn't slam the door in his face, he followed her into the kitchen area, where she immediately headed for the coffee machine. Using the side of her fist, she hit the button to turn it on and checked the level of the water and the beans. She looked as if she'd had less sleep than he had, and he'd had, well, none.

'I'm really sorry about last night, Aisha.' God, did she hear the sincerity in his voice? He hoped so.

'Apologising means nothing if you don't change your actions, Pasco.'

He winced at her freezer-cold tone and instantly knew he'd need a miracle because he'd screwed up. Big time.

Five minutes…why hadn't he taken five damn minutes to call her? What the hell was wrong with him?

Aisha walked past his legs to open the fridge, but his arm shot out and he pulled her to stand between his legs, resting his forehead on her flat stomach. God, she smelled good, her scent cutting through the smell of smoke in his nose.

'Pasco's burned down last night,' he bluntly told her. 'The fire started just after five, we got it under control around eight, eight-thirty.'

When she stepped back, he noticed her eyes were wide with shock. 'Pasco's burnt down?'

He rubbed a hand over his eyes. 'You really didn't know? I thought you would've heard by now—news travels fast in this valley.'

'I've only been here for two months. I'm not plugged into the gossip line,' Aisha explained, her eyes reflecting sympathy and shock. 'I'm so sorry. When? How?'

Pasco filled her in on the details and by the time he was finished, his coffee was cold. Needing the caffeine hit, he put his cup under the spout of the coffee machine and blasted it with steam. 'Between you and me, I think it was Jason.'

Aisha's eyebrows flew up. 'Jason? The guy you recently let go?'

'Yeah.'

'You think he set fire to your place because you fired him?'

'And because I laid criminal charges against him for theft,' Pasco told her, his voice hard. 'He's a hothead, I can easily see him getting drunk and doing something stupid like this. And the fire, so they think, started in the office area. It burned hottest there.

'Didn't you hear me tell you about the fire when I called you last night?' Pasco asked, gripping the bridge of his nose.

She shook her head. 'No, I heard the noise in the background but not much else. You called from someone else's phone.'

'I used my brother's,' he replied, wincing when he remembered the many text messages and missed call alerts that came through when his phone was recharged. 'I tried to call you later, but your phone was off.'

'I switched it off when I left the restaurant,' Aisha said, her tone flat.

Of course she had, and he didn't blame her. He looked at her and shook his head. Despite her hurt, despite him treating her like an after-thought, sympathy brimmed in her eyes. He was starting to think—*know and believe*—he wasn't good enough for her, that he could never make her happy.

The thing was, he was like his dad…selfish, hyper-focused, ruthlessly determined. Okay, he made good monetary decisions instead of bad, combined the determination he inherited from his father with extreme hard work, but at their essence, they were the same. Selfish, relentless, rigid. And both he and his dad had the ability to fall in love with a woman far too good for them. Pasco felt his stomach turn into a lead ball, nausea climbing up his throat. He couldn't help noticing his muscles seemed to be losing strength, that his hands were trembling.

Aisha needed to be his priority, for him to put her first, but as last night proved, when the chips were down, he was too much like his father and unable to put her first. He couldn't keep hurting her—it was unacceptable. He rubbed the back of his head, not sure what to say, to do. He couldn't walk away, but neither could he stay. He wanted to bury himself inside her, lose himself in the taste of her mouth and the softness and fragrance of her skin, but he'd lost the right to touch her.

He stood in no man's land, unable to step forward, and he couldn't go back. He dropped his head, conscious of the burning sensation in his throat, his wetter than normal eyes.

Aisha placed her cup on the dining table and gripped the back of a chair with white-knuckled fingers. He had to look at her, noticing her brown eyes looked darker than usual. Her face was a couple of shades paler, and her mouth was flat with unhappiness.

She lifted her eyes to meet his and slowly shook her head. He braced himself.

'When we first met, I told myself, told you, that we needed some rules, some guidelines to deal with each other. I told myself not to get involved with you, not to let the past colour the future. I didn't listen.'

To be fair, he'd had the same thoughts, but neither did he listen to his inner voice.

'I can't do this, Pasco.'

Her words were what he'd been expecting since first realising that he'd stood her up last night. She wasn't his young wife any more. She was a vibrant, smart woman who knew her own mind and he knew he'd pushed her too far, tested her limits, run out of chances. And he refused to hide behind the fire, use it as an excuse…he'd messed up. Badly. And he'd probably, because he was his father's son, do it again.

Unacceptable.

He was done with hurting her. And if that meant walking away, then that was what he would do.

Pasco stared at her with haunted eyes, his face pale and drawn. That he was physically exhausted was obvious, but Aisha knew he was dancing on the edge of mental exhaustion too. And so, honestly, was she.

They kept knocking the stuffing out of each other, hurting each other, coming close to making it work, but never quite getting it right. It was time to give up, to stop trying. She couldn't take much more Pasco-induced pain.

Or any, really.

Pasco didn't respond to her I-can't-do-this statement, but pain flashed in his eyes and he flinched. Thinking she needed to give him an explanation, she ploughed on, her voice high and tight.

'This dinner seemed to be important to you and it was damn important to me, despite its awful timing. I blew off a meal with the chairman of my company's board to rush back to Cape Town, Pasco! My dinner invitation was a big deal because Mr Lintel never socialises with the common folk. I told Miles, his daughter, that I couldn't go, that I had a date. She understood, she's good like that…she's big into having a balanced life,' Aisha explained.

Pasco flinched and she knew her verbal jab landed on target.

'The strategy session ran over, and I had to excuse myself, something I don't like to do, especially when I'm up for promotion. Anyway, I barely made my flight. Then it was delayed. I tried to call you, but it just rang. I couldn't get hold of you so I rushed from the airport to the restaurant, but you weren't there… Look, I'm sorry about your restaurant, but I'm so damn angry with you, I'm not going to lie.'

Her anger didn't matter, she could nurse it, and her soul-deep hurt, later. She needed to get this out, get it over with and move on.

It's self-care, Aisha, another set of boundaries. You're protecting yourself and you're allowed to do that.

She lifted her hands. 'I'm done, Pasco. Done with wishing that things will change. I know they won't.'

She closed her eyes and shook her head. 'I am not and never will be a priority in your life. Being busy, gathering businesses and bank accounts and trust, making sure that you are nothing like your father is all that's important to you!'

Something in his eyes, a flash of disagreement, but he didn't speak, just kept looking at her with those intense green eyes. For the second time in her life, she was going to walk away from the only man she'd ever loved and, although she knew it was the right thing for her to do, she didn't know if she could bear it. Spots danced in front of her vision and Aisha knew there was a good chance she'd break down completely and beg him to stay.

No... Boundaries. Self-care. Protection.

'Do you know what I realised last night?' she quietly asked. She echoed his body language and folded her arms against her chest, surreptitiously pinching the inside of her arm, directing her mental attention and her pain onto that spot on the tender skin.

'What?' he croaked.

'In trying to be exactly the opposite of your dad, you've turned out to be more like him than you thought.' Distaste flashed across his face, and she was sorry to be the one who hurt him, but he needed to hear the truth. Or the truth the way she saw it.

'You told me that your dad made a habit of reaching for every shiny object that passed by, that he wanted what he wanted, when he wanted it, not caring who it hurt.'

Tumultuous emotions roiled through his eyes and Aisha expected him to respond, to deny her accusation, but, to her surprise, he didn't. He just held her eyes and gestured for her to continue.

'You reach for shiny objects too, Pasco, but yours are work and success and accolades, things to remind you that you are nothing like him. But they are still shiny and you reaching for them still hurts the people who love you, people like me. You'd rather work, intent on gathering money and things, because in doing that you can tell yourself that you're not like him, that you are a success. But in doing that, you're hurting the woman who loves you, the woman who's always loved you, just like your dad hurt your mum. He lost all the money and business, you win it all, but your wives are the ones to suffer.'

Pasco was statute still, his body rigid with tension. All the colour leached from his skin and his eyes were emerald green in his haggard face.

'Jesus! Would you say something, please?' she half shouted, half begged.

Beg me to be yours, tell me you love me...say something to persuade me that you are worth taking a chance on!

He opened his mouth, but slammed it closed again and shook his head. He forced his shoulders up and let them fall, heavy as sin. 'You're right.'

Aisha glared at him. 'That's all you have to say?'

He shrugged again and for the first time, Aisha wanted to hurt him, to shock him into speaking, mentally screaming at him to say or do something to fight for her, to fight for them.

She waited a good twenty seconds, then another twenty, refusing to drop her eyes, to break his stare. Pasco didn't speak.

Right, enough now.

Aisha's voice turned hard. 'I was weak before, Pasco, but I'm not weak any more. I don't need you to provide a life for me, I'm not impressed by your success or your money. I have my career, my own money. I love you, I do, but I can't be with you because I need more than you can give. I need your time. I need you to be present. I need you to *see* me.'

'I *do* see you.'

His words, rough and low, came too late, and were far from convincing. 'You don't, Pasco, not really. You don't see me as an equal part-

ner, someone you're willing to put first, someone you want to put above your need to prove
to yourself that you are a better man than your
father. Everybody but you knows that, by the
way,' she told him.

'I spent my entire childhood not being seen or
respected, being dismissed. I won't tolerate that
from you, or any man. I refuse to stand on the
outside of your life, only to be pulled in when
it suits you.'

Aisha forced herself to walk over to him,
to touch his cheek with the tips of her fingers.
'Miles has offered to send someone to help me
with setting up the restaurant. I think I'm going
to accept her offer and let Kendall work with
you. You'll enjoy her, she's fun.'

He shook his head, and for a moment, just a
moment, she thought he was holding his arms
tight across his chest to keep from reaching
for her.

'I'm sorry, Aish. I really am,' he managed
to croak.

Aisha released a small sob, shook her head
and forced herself to walk away.

A long, miserable week later, Pasco stood in the
empty warehouse in New York City, trying to
ignore his throbbing, aching heart. Hank was
rambling on about capacity and seating, telling

him how eager the city was for a new restaurant, how the eating scene had changed since Covid-19. He wasn't paying attention, and only heard every fifth word he said.

All he could think about was Aisha's words. *'You reach for shiny objects too, Pasco, but yours are work and success and accolades, things to remind you that you are nothing like him...that you are a success.'*

A successful businessman, maybe, but not a good human being. He was, in many ways, his father's son and that was a problem and his biggest challenge. He didn't want to be that driven, hyper-focused jerk he'd been.

So why was he here? In New York? He didn't want to live in this city, work a thousand hours a week, be the lauded New York City success story again.

Be honest, Kildare, you're only in Manhattan because it hurt too much to stay in Cape Town. To even be in the same area as Aisha. Because you hoped that flying to New York and listening to Hank's pitch would be a distraction from the suffocating pain and relief from the heavy stone squashing your heart.

God, he missed Aisha. He felt as if he were missing an arm, a leg, his damned spine. The last time they split, he dived into work, focusing his energy on building his empire. This time around, work failed to hold his interest.

After booking into the Waldorf, he'd left again immediately and started walking the city that had been his home for five years. He'd walked for hours and hours, eventually stopping outside the premises of his old restaurant, now an upmarket deli.

He'd earned the first of his Michelin stars there, been lauded for bringing innovative dishes to the jaded food scene. He'd been featured in food magazines and on travel programmes, in fact, his appearance on a travel programme had led to him having his own.

He'd had royalty and rogues eat his food, celebrities of all sizes, shapes, and sorts. His reviews were generally good, and he'd earned many tens of millions feeding the great and good, and not so good, of this magnificent city.

He definitely didn't need to do it again. Pasco looked at Hank, who hadn't taken a breath since jumping into the cab that had brought them here. He wore a thick gold chain around his neck, another on his wrist, and a fat Rolex. Hank had a magnificent apartment overlooking Central Park, ate out every night, and had a different girlfriend every month. He was a billionaire investor, another collector of shiny objects like businesses and bitcoin.

'I'm telling ya, Pasco, we can make ourselves a fortune.'

He already had a fortune, and that was before he counted the money he'd placed in trusts for his family. He still owned an apartment in New York, another in London, a villa in Greece, and his two homes in South Africa. Apart from his restaurants, he owned a couple of industrial properties and a block of apartments, all of which generated rental income. He received money from his range of kitchen accessories, interest from his fat bank accounts.

'You and I can do great things together. More great things,' Hank amended, smiling. Pasco jammed his hands in the pockets of his suit trousers and looked at the older man.

'Why did you never marry, Hank?' he demanded.

Hank frowned at his out-of-the-blue question. 'Too much hassle, not enough time,' he eventually answered. 'Truth be told, I love my work more than I could ever love a woman. We're the same, you and I.'

Pasco flinched at the observation. Were they? He loved to work, loved his job but…

But he loved Aisha more. None of it meant anything without her. She was what was missing from the life, the empty hole he couldn't fill because it was Aisha-shaped, and the only one able to complete him. So, yeah, if he had to choose between work and her, it would be her. Funny how it took making a complete idiot of himself and flying halfway across the world to look at an opportunity he had no interest in to come to that realisation.

'It's not for me, Hank,' Pasco said, looking around. For someone else, sure, but not him. New York wasn't his place any more; he didn't want to move back here, commit to working fourteen-hour days for the next ten or so years.

Hank didn't miss a beat. 'Okay, what will suit you?'

He had no idea; maybe it was a small restaurant, with simple dishes prepared well, great wine, greenhouses, and herb gardens, maybe not, but it wasn't here, across the pond away from Aisha. What would really suit him was his ring on her finger, his son running into his arms, Aisha's stomach round with their second child.

Maybe it was even doing what he did now, but slowing down, delegating, occasionally taking his hands off the wheel, but always, always going home to Aisha.

What would suit him best was a life that worked for Aisha, with him at her side.

He needed to spend his life being there for her, spending time with her, supporting her, *seeing* her. Making her his sole priority because she was the most important person in his life, ensuring she never felt on the outside looking in again.

Whatever she wanted from him, he'd give to her. She could work, not work, jump in and out of his life—he didn't care!—as long as she was happy, fulfilled, living her best life.

God, he needed to talk to her, to find a way to make this work. He'd been hyper-focused all his life, but winning Aisha back would be the biggest, hardest, most important battle of his life. 'Well, what do you want, Pasco?'

Pasco pulled up a smile for Hank. 'I want to go home, Hank. I want to drink wine with my woman, look at the mountains, smell the fynbos. New York isn't for me any more.'

Pasco felt his phone vibrate and pulled it out of the inside pocket of his jacket, his eyebrows lifting when he saw Muzi video calling him.

'What's up, dude?'

Muzi, as he always did when he was excited, babbled away in Xhosa. 'Ro's in labour! I'm going to be a dad!'

Pasco's heart jumped and he silently cursed. What the hell was he doing here when all the people he cared about were on another continent, eighteen hours away? 'Oh, man, Muzi, that's so exciting!' he responded in rusty Xhosa. God, his accent was dreadful.

Muzi obviously thought so too because he

switched to English. 'She keeps saying that it might be a false alarm, that it's a practice round, Braxton somethings, but I know this is it, Pas. I'm going to be a dad!'

'You are,' Pasco told him, grinning. This was the first good news he'd had all week, the first thing to make him smile. 'I'm heading straight to the airport and I'll leave as soon as I can. Send me a picture as soon as they are born, and I'll come straight to the hospital, okay?'

'Okay.' Muzi placed a hand on his heart. 'I'm not ready for this, Pas.'

Pasco walked to the exit and stepped into the sunshine. But it wasn't tip of Africa sunshine, so it felt wrong. 'You are ready, brother, and even if you weren't, they are on their way. Hang in there, Muzi, and keep me updated, okay?'

'Digby is on his way, so is Keane. And Radd. But I need—'

He needed him, his best friend. Yeah, Pasco didn't need him to spell it out. He needed to get home, to meet the twins, and to share a cigar with his oldest friend.

But even more important than that, he needed to find Aisha and love her for the rest of her life.

CHAPTER TWELVE

THE NEXT DAY, in her cottage, Aisha yanked a bottle of wine out of her fridge and held the cool bottle to her forehead. Lowering it, she squinted at the bottle, saw it was nearly empty, and cursed. She lived in one of the premier wine areas of the world and all she had to drink, after a fairly crappy day, was a few gulps of wine.

Oh, well, it was better than nothing. Dashing the minuscule amount into a glass, she considered what she could eat for supper, realised she still hadn't bought any food, and decided she wasn't hungry.

Well, she was hungry for junk food…she could murder a packet of fries, slam down a huge bar of chocolate. Emotional eating, Aisha?

Sure, she was allowed since she was feeling so damn emotional!

Taking her wine back to the living area of her cottage, she curled up into the corner of the couch and started scrolling through her social media accounts. Her oldest nephew was a chess champion; Hema had been invited to speak at a conference in Germany; Reyka posted a photo of her and her husband.

They looked pretty and perfect and she didn't care. For the first time in a long time, she could shake off the feelings of insecurity and stop judging her life by her sisters' accomplishments and milestones. She had an amazing career, she did good work and her boss valued her. There was a good chance she'd still get the promotion she so wanted. But unlike her siblings, she was nearly thirty and not married, a big black mark.

No, stop! Not being married wasn't a problem, nor a sin. It was perfectly okay for her to be single...

And apparently, so was confronting her mother. That awful telephonic conversation a week or so ago had actually resulted in her and her parents sitting down for a one-on-one meal two nights ago. It had been awkward and uncomfortable, but they'd tried and for that Aisha couldn't be more grateful. She was sure their next get-together would be easier and, in time, maybe she could even reboot her relationships with her sisters. She would never match their intellectual brilliance, but she no longer felt the need to; she was Aisha and she had value.

Her relationship with Reyka was beyond repair and she was okay with letting it go or, in the interest of family unity, being polite but having as little to do with her as possible.

Aisha scrolled through more social media posts, stopping when she saw a photo posted by Ro an hour before.

She sat in a hospital bed, looking tired and pale, her hair a mess, but her eyes glowing with happiness. She held a baby wrapped in a blue blanket in each arm, and her smile could power a nuclear plant. Aisha lifted her hand to her mouth, tears stinging her eyes. She tapped her screen and saw more photos, Muzi kissing her forehead, his eyes closed, a tear on his cheek. Muzi holding his boys, his eyes dancing with excitement. Another picture of Muzi showing his boys to the Tempest-Vanes and other people she didn't know. Aisha stared at the photograph, looking for Pasco. He wasn't in the photograph…

Why not? Pasco was Muzi's best and oldest friend, and he'd never miss the birth of the twins. Was he okay? Why wasn't he there?

He'd probably just stepped out of the room and missed the photo op. Aisha enlarged the photograph of the twins and smiled at their chubby cheeks, curly hair, and rosebud mouths. Both had Muzi's deep, brown-black eyes.

Aisha placed her hand on her heart, her throat tight with emotion. She was so happy for Ro.

And Muzi. Happy for their friends, the clan she saw on the screen. Because that was what they looked to be, a group who were each other's safety net and support structure. They were wealthy, sure, stupidly so, but they had something money couldn't buy: they were a tribe, a family, knitted together by love.

She wanted a clan like that, a place where she fitted in. A place where she didn't need a PhD, to present academic papers or to save lives. Somewhere she could just be herself...

She needed friends, a community and, when her heart stopped aching and breaking, in a couple of years or decades, she might even look for a man. She didn't expect to experience a wild and intense love affair again—Pasco was a once-in-a-lifetime force of nature—but maybe she could find a companion, friendship with a man she didn't mind seeing naked.

But the thought of living her life, of being with anyone but Pasco made her feel a little, no, a lot, queasy.

It's just a thought, Shetty, not a stone-carved commandment! Jeez...

In the meantime, she'd work, get St Urban up and running and tomorrow she'd brief Kendall, who'd flown into Cape Town this afternoon, on Ro's restaurant project. Miles had all but told her the promotion was hers, so she'd start looking for a little house, probably in Johannesburg so she could be closer to Priya, a place to call her own. She'd keep herself busy and, in time, her battered and shattered heart would piece itself together.

Everything passed, eventually. She just had to hang on until the pain eased, until her tears stopped, until the sun started shining again.

Aisha felt her stomach rumble and told herself she should eat. She didn't want to, but she needed fuel, almost as much as she needed sleep. Both had been in short supply lately. Forcing herself to rise, she wrinkled her nose, wondering what she could push down her tight throat.

In the kitchen, she pulled open her fridge door and scowled at the empty shelves. Cheese, yoghurt...wilted salad. *Ugh.*

A gentle rap on her door had her turning and, grateful for the distraction, she walked back into the lounge, expecting to see Kendall on her doorstep, as her colleague had said she might stop by this evening to say hello.

She pulled the door open and stared into a long-sleeved, navy-blue T-shirt. She dropped her eyes to see the edges of a leather jacket, long legs covered in jeans, and trendy trainers. She tipped her head back, her eyes slamming into his, deep and forest green.

'You're not at the hospital. You're here,' Aisha said, trying to wrap her head around the fact that

Pasco stood outside her front door. Why wasn't he with his best friends and their babies?

She tipped her head to the side. 'Uh, why aren't you at the hospital?'

'After I landed, I popped in, met the twins, and then came straight here.'

'Uh…okay. Why? Everyone you love is there.'

'Except the person I love the most,' he said, lifting one big shoulder. 'It's freezing out here— shall we go inside?'

Aisha nodded, her brain still trying to catch up to reality. When her feet remained glued to the spot, her eyes stuck on his, Pasco put his hands under her forearms and easily lifted her. Walking her backwards, he deposited her inside the cottage and kicked the door shut with his foot.

Looking down at her, he shed his leather bomber-style jacket and tossed his car keys onto the surface of the small table to the side of the door.

'Hi,' he said, his thumb skating across her cheekbone.

'Hi back,' Aisha whispered.

Aisha turned and, feeling a little shaky, sat down on the edge of the grey couch. She pulled a yellow cushion onto her lap and hugged it. She gestured to the chair opposite her and watched as Pasco sat. He immediately leaned forward and rested his forearms on his thighs.

'You said you landed. Where were you?' she asked.

'New York,' Pasco told her, his eyes not leaving hers.

She lifted her eyebrows. 'Why were you in New York?'

And why are you here?

Lifting his head, he nailed her with an intense look. 'I was there because I was looking at setting up another restaurant. My investor, Hank, found a property and it has potential for an amazing restaurant.'

Aisha's heart dropped to her toes and her blood turned to ice water. She wrapped her arms around her torso and started to shiver. He was going back to the States and, in doing that, hammered the last nail into their already sealed-tight coffin. Why was she surprised and why, oh, why had she expected anything different? She hauled in a deep breath and forced herself to smile. 'Sounds interesting.'

'It's a great space but not for me. Neither is the city.'

She frowned, trying to keep up. 'I don't understand.'

'Another restaurant, anywhere but here, is... how did you put it? A shiny object that I have to have,' Pasco explained, his smile forced. She saw his worried expression and it was his lack of confidence, his hesitation, that kick-started her brain. She'd never seen him looking unsure, uncertain. She didn't like it.

'You were right, I have spent my life doing everything I can to prove to myself that I'm not my father's son. But in trying to be the opposite of him, I became more like him than I imagined. I look like him, talk like him, but I *am* not him. I refuse to be,' Pasco stated, his eyes flashing with intense emotion.

No, he wasn't, not really. Oh, parts of him were, but he was a better guy than his father had ever been. He was the guy who worked hard, who gave his everything, supported his friends, made her feel more alive than she ever had before.

'I just want to be with you, Aish. I'll be a good partner, I promise. I'll give you copies of all my bank accounts and never ask you about yours. I'll change nappies and cook and we will make every major decision together. We'll argue, probably, but I swear I'll listen and I'll always, *always* respect your point of view. I'll respect you.'

It was his turn to ramble, and she found it sweet.

She was about to speak, but Pasco beat her to it. 'I'll move. I'll hand over complete control of Pasco's at The Vane to my chef de cuisine and I won't rebuild Pasco's, Franschhoek. If you get the promotion, I'll move to London or Johannesburg. If you don't get the promotion, I'll follow you wherever you go next.'

Aisha's fingers dug into the fabric of the cushion, and she was sure her eyebrows had reached her hairline. 'Are you offering to give up your career? For me?'

Pasco nodded. 'I'm not saying it will be easy and I'll probably be, on occasion, an ass about it, but if that's what it takes, then I'll do it.'

'But why?'

His eyes drilled into her, almost begging her to understand. 'Because your job is important to you. You've worked hard to establish your career and you love your work. But you are my priority, your happiness is my *only* priority. You're the most important person in my life, hell, you *are* my life.'

And there it was. God, it was sweeter and sexier and more wonderful than she could ever have imagined. But despite her need to throw her arms around him and taste his lovely mouth and lay her hands on all his skin-covered muscles, they still needed to talk.

Be an adult, Shetty. You can get to the fun stuff later.

Pasco released a low, frustrated growl. 'I wish you'd say something, Aisha.'

She mulled over a few sentences, discarded

them, considered others. 'I don't want or need you to give up your career or your business for me, Pasco, that was *never* the point. I just wanted to feel I was as important to you, that I had an equal call on your time.' Aisha smiled at the hint of relief she saw in his eyes.

Yeah, Pasco not working would drive them both mad. His thumb skimmed her cheekbone. 'I promise you will never doubt that, or me, again.'

He started to move off his chair, but Aisha held up her hand, silently telling him to stay there. He slumped back and stared at her, his expression a little frustrated. 'Can we have make-up sex now?' he asked.

Aisha smiled, knowing he was trying to lift the tension a notch or two. 'Not yet. I still have things to say.'

Pasco hauled in a breath and straightened his shoulders as if bracing himself to take another verbal beating.

'When you walked inside, you said you loved me. Is that true?' she asked, discarding her pillow and wrapping her hands around her knee.

Pasco nodded. 'I do.'

Two words, so simple, so powerful.

Aisha blinked away the moisture in her eyes. 'I love you too.'

He lunged in her direction, but she laughed

and edged down the couch. 'Not yet! Just hold on, okay?'

Pasco glanced at his watch. 'You've got two minutes, talk fast.'

'I'm still up for promotion—if I get it, I'll move to Cape Town. I don't want to stop working and I won't let you stop either, so we will need to adjust our schedules.'

'Done.' He easily agreed. 'A part of me wants to slow down, take it easy, just be. Be with you.' Those were the sweetest words she'd ever heard.

'But we need to make some rules…' he added.

Aisha mock-frowned at him, her lips twitching with amusement. 'You're not good at rules, Pas.'

'I am when I make them,' he told her, cupping her cheek. 'One rule, two parts…we always prioritise each other, and our kids, above work. That's non-negotiable.'

'Agreed.'

'And we make every important decision together. Deal?'

Aisha nodded enthusiastically. 'Deal.'

He smiled at her before looking at his watch. 'We still have a minute and ten seconds left.' His mouth tipped up in that sexy smile she so adored. 'Anything else we need to cover or can I strip you naked now?'

There was just one more thing…

She had a man who loved her, who'd promised

to put her first, offered to give up his business for her, someone who *saw* her clearly. He was a good man, not perfect—perfection was over-rated, and she was far from perfect herself—but he was perfect for her.

She pulled in some much-needed air. 'Will you marry me again, Pas? Love me every day and in every way, give me babies and back rubs? Will you talk to me and fight with me and consult with me? Will you build me up when I'm feeling small and pull me back into line when I'm being awful?'

'You're never awful,' Pasco told her, and Aisha swallowed at the look of adoration on his face.

'That wasn't a yes,' Aisha told him on a wobbly laugh. God, maybe she was going too fast again. They'd only been back in each other's lives for a couple of months—maybe she was jumping the gun again, maybe it was too soon. What was she thinking? Talk about history repeating itself...

'I'm sorry, I'm rushing things, rushing you,' Aisha said, waving her hands around.

Pasco moved over to the couch and sat down on the coffee table in front of her and placed his hands on her knees. 'Look at me, sweetheart.'

Aisha raised her head and sucked in her breath when she saw his face. His eyes were tender, his mouth curling in a pleased smile, his fingers warm on her thighs. 'Sure,' he stated, sounding completely confident.

Great, but… 'What are you agreeing to, Pas?'

He curled his big hand around her neck and lowered his forehead to hers. 'Everything,' he whispered. 'And a whole lot more,' he added.

She brushed her lips against his before pulling back. 'One more thing?'

'Make it quick,' he muttered, placing kisses on her jaw.

'Let's not keep our relationship or our marriage a secret this time around, okay? Love needs to stand in the light, not the dark.'

Pasco pulled his phone from the back pocket of his jeans and swiped his thumb across the screen.

'What are you doing, Kildare?' Aisha demanded, caught between laughter and frustration.

He held up a finger and punched the keyboard. He lifted the phone, took a photo of her, and looked down at his screen again. Then he handed her his phone and she looked down at the screen, seeing her messy hair, broad smile, and happy eyes.

She read the series of one-line messages he sent to the group Family and Friends.

My fiancée.

We're getting married.

Again.

You're invited to the wedding.

Aww...

Pasco whipped the phone out of her hand and typed another message before flinging it onto the couch and standing up. As he bent down to pick her up, she read his words and grinned.

Love her madly. Will answer all questions later.

Much, much later.

* * * * *

Couldn't put
The Rules of Their Red-Hot Reunion *down?*
Don't miss these other Joss Wood stories!

How to Undo the Proud Billionaire
How to Win the Wild Billionaire
How to Tempt the Off-Limits Billionaire

Available now!